SAVAGE SEASON

A DALTON SAVAGE MYSTERY

BOOK 7

L.T. RYAN

WITH

BIBA PEARCE

For information contact:

contact@ltryan.com

http://LTRyan.com

https://www.facebook.com/groups/1727449564174357

THE DALTON SAVAGE SERIES

Savage Grounds

Scorched Earth

Cold Sky

The Frost Killer

Crimson Moon

Dust Devil

Savage Season

Snow Burn

Join the L.T. Ryan reader family & receive a free copy of the Rachel Hatch story, *Fractured*. Click the link below to get started:

https://ltryan.com/rachel-hatch-newsletter-signup-1

ONE

WHY DID Halloween always turn people into idiots?

It was nearly ten o'clock, and the phones at the sheriff's department hadn't stopped ringing all evening. The team had been in and out non-stop.

Fireworks in the south end of town. Teenagers throwing eggs at storefronts on Main. A complaint about a man dressed as a chainsaw murderer chasing kids outside the gas station. Two loose dogs in skeleton costumes tearing through a church pumpkin display.

Somewhere near Cottonwood Drive, someone had set off what sounded suspiciously like dynamite, although Savage suspected it was just Tanner Lowe and his idiot cousins getting creative again.

He stood in the middle of the office, an empty coffee cup in his hand, listening to Barb field calls from the front desk. Barbara Wright was the department's administrator, and a pretty efficient one at that. She ran a tight ship, but she also kept an eye on the team, making sure they were okay.

"Tell him no, Doris," she said into the phone with the grim patience of a woman who had long ago made peace with the ridiculous shenanigans of the local community. "The sheriff is not going to arrest a twelve-year-old for toilet-papering your junipers." She listened, then rolled her eyes. "Because it's Halloween, Doris."

Savage hid a smile and went to grab a refill from the break room next door to the squad room.

He thought about his son, Connor, who would be asleep by now. Becca had sent a photo earlier of him dressed as a pumpkin, grinning with his four teeth on show. Savage sighed as he headed back to his office. Damn, he missed them.

The radio squawked. Barb answered.

"Bonfire's getting rowdy," Deputy Becky Sinclair's voice shouted over the ambient noise. "The Angels have arrived. Might need some backup."

"Tell her I'm on my way," he said to Barb, downing his new coffee in one.

The Crimson Angels were an outlaw biker gang who claimed they had gone legit. In her mid-forties, Rosalie Weston had taken over after usurping her now late husband, Axel Weston. It was more of a hostile takeover, but Savage had to give the woman her due. She had guts.

Under her rule, the MC had been more structured, more controlled, and collectively, had done less jail time than when her husband had been in charge. Overall, it was a welcome change, and an arrangement he could live with.

He grabbed his keys and checked his weapon before heading outside. It was mostly dark, the sun having set about an hour ago. In the west, a faint orange glow lingered just above the horizon, but it didn't offer much in the way of light.

The streetlamps had come on, but Main was pretty well lit by fairy lights, jack-o-lanterns and eerie glows emanating from decorated shop windows. A banner strung across the street, that had begun to sag in the middle, read *Hawk's Landing Harvest Festival* in bright, orange lettering.

The town had made an effort this year. People needed something to celebrate, something fun and seasonal, so the decorations had gone up a little earlier and the festivities were a little more boisterous.

He could still detect the anxiety that sat quietly beneath the surface, though. The wildfires that had burned through forty thousand acres of mountain forest above the town in the summer had left an ugly scar on the hillsides and in the hearts of the community. It would take time to heal.

Kids in costumes hurtled down the street, screeching and laughing. He watched them turn into the lot next door where the Methodist church had set up a trunk-or-treat stop. A tiny astronaut dragged a plastic pumpkin bucket twice the size of his head behind him, and the familiar longing hit Savage again. He sucked in a breath of cool air and tried not to think about his family.

Some nights they managed a call. Some nights they didn't. He got up to Pagosa Springs between cases, usually spent a couple of days living out of a nearby motel. It wasn't ideal, but it was better than not seeing them at all. He had to be content with that. For now.

Savage drove into the center of town and parked as close to the green as possible, hoping to deter any would-be troublemakers. He could smell the bonfire before he'd even gotten out of the Suburban.

Leaving the lights flashing, he strode across the lawn to where Sinclair stood, hands on her hips, watching a group of bikers laughing and jeering.

He recognized a couple of them. It wasn't the entire posse, thank God, but these few could cause enough trouble on their own.

The argument seemed to be over a scantily clad woman dressed as a witch, complete with green body paint. Fighting over her were a scar-faced Freddy Kreuger and two of the bikers.

"Don't be a spoil sport," the woman told the man dressed as Freddy. "They were only being friendly."

"Yeah, that's us. Friendly," the biker with the beer gut and leather waistcoat jeered.

Freddy tensed, balling his hands into fists.

"Come on, Len. Let's get out of here. The pigs have arrived." His buddy, tattooed with long, scraggly hair and a baseball cap, tried to grab his arm.

Beer Gut shrugged him off. “No way, man. I’m busy flirtin’ here.”

“She’s not interested,” Freddy took a menacing step forward. In the firelight, he looked quite terrifying. A small child screamed and ran back to its parents.

Sinclair turned and grimaced. “It’s about to kick off.”

Savage nodded and was about to step in when Freddy threw a punch.

Beer Gut retaliated. Freddy stumbled backwards, narrowly avoiding falling over a couple of teens sitting on a blanket nearby.

“Hey. Watch it, dumbass!” one of them called.

“You watch it,” Beer Gut retorted, then laughed as if he’d said something really smart.

Freddy got up and charged. Savage heard the air expel from Beer Gut’s, well, gut, before he stumbled backwards into his friend.

The friend lost it and careened into Freddy. The witch screamed and jumped on the second biker’s back, wrapping her green arms around his neck and her legs around his waist.

“Oh, Lord,” Sinclair muttered, and ran over to pull her off.

Savage grabbed Beer Gut, who was about to punch the living daylights out of Freddy, who lay on the ground bleeding from what looked like a broken nose, although it was hard to tell amongst all the face paint.

“Get off him!” Sinclair yelled, tugging the woman free.

“Yeah, get off me, you crazy bitch,” biker number two complained.

“Hey!” Sinclair reprimanded him. “Watch your language, buster, or I’ll arrest your ass as well.” She snapped cuffs on the witch.

“What did I do?” the witch complained, black hair falling over her pouting red lips.

“Try assault,” Sinclair snapped back, leading her away from the group.

“Ha! Take that,” the biker jeered after them.

Savage had Beer Gut in cuffs, and was about to go after Freddy, who held up his hands. "I was just protecting my woman. I want to press charges."

"Then you'll have to come down to the station to do it," Savage barked, turning towards his vehicle. "When you've sobered up. Unless you want to be arrested for a DUI."

He stopped.

Idiot.

"Thank you, Sheriff," called one of the teens.

He shot them a stiff nod as he walked past, biker in tow.

Rosalie would no doubt be down at the station in the morning posting bail. How she controlled this unruly bunch, he had no idea. He was just glad somebody did.

TWENTY MINUTES LATER, he'd just driven into the sally port beneath the sheriff's office to unload his prisoner when the radio squawked.

"Hey, Sheriff?"

He recognized his deputy, Lucas McBride's voice.

"Yeah. Go ahead, Lucas."

"We've got a situation down on Maple Ridge Lane."

Savage could tell by the grim tone of his deputy's voice that it was serious.

"What kind of situation?"

"A bad one. You'd better come down here."

He didn't like the sound of that.

"On my way."

Turning around, he said to the biker. "Let's go. I've got somewhere to be."

The biker grunted and waited until Savage opened the back door and hauled him out. The heavy metal-coated garage doors ground down behind them. Sinclair wasn't there with her culprit yet, but she would be soon.

Savage entered his code into the keypad and waited for the lock to click open. Then he led the biker inside. Thorpe, who would have seen him drive in on the monitor, was there to meet them.

Savage handed the biker to his deputy. "Process this guy. I've got to head out. Lucas called in an incident."

Thorpe gave a nod and took the biker by the arm. "Sure thing. Call if you need assistance."

Savage spun and strode out again, back to his truck.

THE DRIVE to Maple Ridge Lane didn't take long, even with the detour on account of the traffic around the green. It was a quiet residential street on the eastern edge of town.

Savage saw his deputy's cruiser parked outside a modest ranch-style home set back from the road. The porch light cut the dark, and a grinning pumpkin with half its head caved in stood on one side beside the front steps. The door was half open.

A crowd had gathered on the sidewalk. Kids with buckets of candy, parents huddled around them with concerned looks on their faces.

Off to one side, wrapped in blankets over their costumes, stood a couple of youngsters—one dressed as a pirate and the other as a vampire. They were crying, and an adult stood nearby on a cell phone. Trying to locate the parents, no doubt.

Savage got out of the SUV and approached Lucas, who stood out front, a grim expression on his chiseled face. He had the solid, ready look that Savage had come to depend on. Square jaw, broad shoulders, a competent air that came from being in the Marines for many years prior to this job.

"What's happened?" Savage asked.

"Double homicide," Lucas kept his voice low. "Apparently they're the couple who live here." He nodded behind him to the house. "Couple of kids found the bodies."

"Shit," Savage muttered.

"Yeah. It's not pretty. The neighbor is trying to call their folks to come get them."

"You talked to them?" he asked, pulling a pair of crime scene gloves out of his pocket.

A nod. "The door was open, so they thought that meant they could go in and help themselves to candy."

"Jesus." Savage snapped on the gloves.

From where he was standing, the interior of the house looked warm and welcoming. The hall light was on, and somewhere in the background he could hear music playing. Sounded like an old country song.

"Who are they?" he asked as they headed up the path toward the house.

"Frank and Sarah Wilson," Lucas supplied. "Lived here for over thirty years."

Savage felt heaviness in his chest, the way he always did when he was about to walk into a crime scene. "Burglary?"

Lucas just gestured to the door. "The lock was forced."

Savage gave it a quick inspection on the way in. "Doesn't look that robust to begin with."

Lucas shrugged. "Long-time residents. Guess they felt safe."

To be fair, this was usually a pretty safe neighborhood. Lots of middle-aged and retired folks lived out here. There was more space, the houses were bigger, and they were still only a couple of miles from the downtown area.

The entry hall opened onto a living area decorated for the season in an old-fashioned way. Ceramic plates on the mantel, a knitted orange throw over the armchair, a bowl of fun-size candy bars over-turned on the rug, bright wrappers scattered like confetti.

A white male, mid-sixties, lay flat on his back near the doorway to the kitchen, one hand curled against his chest. His wife was three feet away by the dining table, in a position that suggested she had turned toward the sound but never finished the motion.

Both had been shot in the head.

TWO

SAVAGE STOOD VERY STILL, taking it all in.

The TV was still on, its flickering light casting pale shadows across the room. That was the source of the country music. Bluegrass, rhythmic and incessant. He found the remote and turned it off.

The silence was a relief. Now he could think.

There were no casings on the floor, nothing disturbed. Nothing seemed out of place, other than the bodies, of course.

"Don't think this was a burglary," he decided.

It wasn't a spur of the moment domestic, or some junkie kicking in the door for cash either. There'd be signs if it was. The place would be ransacked, furniture upended, belongings discarded all over the floor.

There was none of that.

Lucas stood on the periphery, out of Savage's way.

"They've both been shot twice," he said, as Savage crouched beside Frank Wilson. "One beneath the jaw, one at the temple. Whoever did this wasn't messing around."

Savage narrowed his gaze, studying the damage. The wounds

were clean and precise. No mess and hardly any spray. He moved over to Sarah's body. Identical entry points.

Exhaling, he looked up at his deputy. "Double tap."

Lucas gave a tight nod. "Yeah. My guess is this was a professional hit."

Savage straightened, letting that sink in. His gaze fell on the front windows, curtains closed. A lamp glowed softly in the corner. Outside somewhere, a child cried.

"You checked the rest of the house?" he said, after a beat.

"As soon as I got here. It's clear. Other than the front door, there are no signs of entry or exit."

He gave a nod. "The scene needs to be contained until Ray and Pearl can get here." Ray and Pearl Turner served as the department's primary crime scene processing and medical forensic duo. The couple had retired to Hawk's Landing from Denver, seeking a quieter pace of life, but instead worked most of Savage's cases for him.

Ray was a qualified medical examiner, and Pearl an expert in forensics. Together, they had the big city experience he required and could work quickly without the need to wait weeks for results like the other small towns in the area.

"You want me to call Sinclair?"

He thought about it, then shook his head. Sinclair had recently gotten engaged to O'Riley, Hawk's Landing's fire chief, so he didn't want to monopolize too much of her time. "No, leave it for now. We can manage." She'd be dealing with the two detainees in the cells anyway, before clocking out for the night.

Lucas pulled out his phone and left the room. Savage turned back to the bodies.

RAY AND PEARL arrived forty minutes later, their old Ford Taurus rattling up Maple Ridge Lane, its headlights cutting through the dark.

Ray climbed out first and went straight to the trunk where he pulled out a Tyvek suit, an action he'd performed a thousand times before. Pearl followed, camera hanging over her shoulder, holding a large case.

Savage met them out front. "Thanks for coming out here on such short notice."

Ray was already looking towards the house. "Isn't this Frank and Sarah's place? What happened?"

"You know them?" Savage asked, hesitating. Maybe this wasn't such a good idea.

"Sarah's in my book club," Pearl answered, but she maintained her air of professionalism. "Was there some kind of accident?"

The mere fact that Ray and Pearl were here meant they knew the couple were deceased. Whatever emotions they'd felt at hearing the news had been dealt with or shelved.

"Double homicide," he said, softly.

Ray's eyebrows shot up. "Really?"

"That's not what I was expecting," Pearl admitted, heading toward the house.

"If you don't want to—" Savage began, but Pearl just raised a hand.

"Come on, we don't have all night."

Ray met Savage's gaze.

"She'll be all right. She's made of stern stuff."

He nodded and followed them in.

Lucas had cordoned off the house, so they had to duck under the police tape across the front door.

Savage had spoken with the two kids and their respective parents, who'd taken them home. He'd offered therapy, as was standard procedure when kids were involved, but he hoped they wouldn't be too affected by what they'd seen. Ironically, it was no worse than some of the costumes he'd seen tonight.

Pearl stopped in the hallway, gaze fixed on the bodies of the two people she'd known, but it was only for a moment. Then, mouth set in a determined line, she set down her case, and reached for the camera around her neck. Savage admired her stoicism.

Ray knelt beside Frank Wilson, who Savage guessed had been gunned down first since he was closest to the door, and began his examination. While he worked, Pearl moved through the room, methodically photographing everything from multiple angles.

Savage stood back and watched, his hands in his jacket pockets, letting them do their thing. After ten minutes or so, he said, "Cause of death is clearly the double gunshot wounds."

Ray straightened up. "Double tap, both victims. Same placement each time—submandibular and temple." He indicated the points on his own jaw and head with two fingers. "Clean, controlled, and identical. There's no variation at all between the two, which tells you something about the shooter's discipline and training."

"Pro?" Savage asked.

"Definitely. This wasn't done in the heat of the moment. It's way too precise." He leaned in again, studying the wounds more closely. "Small, clean entries. No tearing or fragmentation. That's not cheap ammo." He glanced up at Savage. "I'd put money on a nine-mil. Probably bonded duty rounds. The kind designed to go in clean and do the job properly."

Pearl had put down her camera and was now on her hands and knees looking around the body.

"No casings," she rested back on her haunches. "Either they were recovered afterward, which would require time and composure at the scene, or the weapon was fitted with a casing capture system."

Savage massaged his temples. This was getting more complex by the second. "That's military grade equipment."

"Not the sort of thing you pick up at a gun show," Ray said with a wry nod. He got to his feet with a slight wince that acknowledged the hard floor and his age.

"I didn't see any security cameras." Pearl lifted a hand so her husband could pull her to her feet. "But that's not surprising knowing Sarah and Frank. They weren't the type."

"There's one on the house across the street, but it points at their own driveway," Savage said. He'd spotted it earlier. Lucas was going door-to-door, asking the neighbors if they'd heard anything, but he wasn't holding his breath.

The properties stood apart from each other, and it was Halloween. Even without silencers, the gunshots might have been mistaken for firecrackers.

Ray shook his head. "I've called for an ambulance. We'll get them to the morgue, and I'll have a better look. But from what I can see, this wasn't random."

"Who would target Frank and Sarah?" Pearl asked, shaking her head. "They were harmless. Wouldn't hurt a fly." Behind her pale blue eyes, Savage saw sadness and a flash of anger.

"Did they have any relatives?"

"I think there's a son, but I'm not sure where," Pearl replied. "Sarah mentioned him a couple of times, but not recently."

Thorpe would find out. They'd have to get the son to come for an official ID.

"I'm sorry," Savage said simply. "Do you know why anyone would want to hurt the Wilsons?"

"I can't think of a single reason."

"I didn't know them that well, but they seemed an affable sort of couple," Ray added. "But someone obviously had a grudge."

Savage took one last look at the bodies. The couple had been cut down in the middle of their evening. The overturned candy bowl indicated they'd been expecting trick-or-treaters. Maybe they'd been enjoying a quiet night in. Regardless, they'd been surprised by someone hellbent on ensuring they didn't make it through another day.

Now he just had to find out why.

THREE

THE COFFEE MACHINE WAS BROKEN.

It had been making a sound like an injured animal for the past week. A deep, rhythmic grinding that everyone had pretended not to notice in the hope that it would resolve itself. This morning, it had finally given up entirely.

It now sat on a table in the break room in a state of obvious and irreversible failure, a ring of brown liquid around its base. Barbara had placed a handwritten sign against it that read OUT OF ORDER in letters large enough to be read from the doorway.

"Dammit," Savage muttered as he returned to his desk. It was going to be a long day without caffeine.

It had been after three in the morning when he'd finally locked up the office and gone home. Lucas had left an hour before him after updating him on the door-to-door neighborhood enquiries.

It was as Savage had thought. Nobody had heard anything suspicious, but then there were plenty of fireworks going off, kids shouting and laughing, and music blaring. Four gunshots, especially from a gun equipped with suppressors, wouldn't make a peep in all that noise.

Sinclair was already at her desk, hair pulled back in a ponytail, shadows under her eyes that suggested she hadn't slept well either. Halloween was always rough, one way or another.

Thorpe wasn't in yet, but he'd been on the night shift, looking after the green witch and Beer Gut, whose real name turned out to be Trevor "My friends call me Torque" Sanders.

Savage had taken over at six and released them a couple of hours later since nobody—not even the irate Freddy Kreuger—had arrived to press charges. The woman had stumbled out, leaving a smudge of green body paint in the cell, while Torque had given him the bird. He'd been tempted to throw him back in just for that.

Lucas strode in and nodded in his direction. "Mornin' Sheriff."

Savage nodded back.

"Hey, Lucas," Sinclair said, looking up. "Coffee machine's broken."

"I know." He grimaced.

The front door opened, and Barbara walked in with a cardboard tray of cups from the Bouncing Bean down the street. There was a collective sigh of relief.

"Oh, thank God." Sinclair held out her hands like an eager child. He noticed she was wearing her engagement ring today. Probably forgot to leave it at home. It wasn't a large diamond, but it sparkled, catching the light when she lifted her hand. "You're a sweetheart."

Barb handed one to Lucas, who grinned at her, and then to Savage, who nodded his thanks. Without a word, she returned to her desk at the front of the office.

Savage perched on the edge of Sinclair's desk, as was his habit when calling a meeting, and waited for the team, minus Thorpe, to settle. Once he had their attention, he ran through the events of the night before.

"While we wait for the autopsy results, and anything Pearl might have discovered at the scene, let's look into Frank and Sarah Wilson. This was a targeted hit. Someone wanted them dead. We need to find out why."

"Neighbors said they were a nice couple," Lucas contributed, leaning back in his chair. "Friendly, didn't cause any problems in the area, kept to themselves for the most part."

Savage nodded. That's what Pearl had told him too.

"Pearl Turner knew the victims," he said to a few raised eyebrows. "Sarah Wilson belonged to her book club."

Sinclair tilted her head. "She say anything else about them?"

"Only what Lucas mentioned. She thought there might be a son somewhere. We need to trace him as a priority and inform him of his parents' murder. He might be able to shed some light onto why anyone would want them dead."

Sinclair nodded.

"Pearl is going through the house today to see if she can find anything suspicious, or anything that might give us an idea why they were killed, but nothing looked like it had been disturbed. This was a quick in and out to take care of business."

"Looks like they were shot from just inside the hallway," Lucas said. "We'll have to wait for ballistics to confirm, but I'd say it was a service-caliber pistol. The fact that the bullets got lodged inside the victims suggests subsonic pistol ammo or a heavier bullet that's common in suppressed setups."

Savage gave a nod, appreciating his in-depth knowledge of firearms.

"At least we still have the bullets," Sinclair murmured. "Let's hope they tell us something about the shooter."

"Or shooters," Lucas said.

They discussed a few more elements of the case before Savage let them get on with their work and went back to his office. He'd just sat down when Barbara buzzed through from her desk. "Dalton, Councilwoman Nancy Monroe is here to see you."

Nancy Monroe. What on earth did she want to see him about?

He frowned. "Send her in."

Councilwoman Monroe, a striking African American woman in her late forties, had taken over the council seat from Royce Beckett three months ago, after Beckett's arrest on charges of money laundering and conspiracy. Charges that had sent a tremor through the town's civic infrastructure which hadn't entirely settled yet.

Savage had met her twice before at council functions he'd been obliged to attend. Both times were brief, with just a few words exchanged, but she'd made it clear she hadn't come to Hawk's Landing to continue anything Beckett had started.

He got to his feet as the door to his office opened and Monroe walked in carrying a leather folio under one arm. She was impeccably dressed in a charcoal wool coat over a dark blouse and wore heels that clacked over the floorboards as she walked.

Savage came around the desk and shook her hand.

"Councilwoman, this is a surprise."

"Morning, Sheriff," she said, as he gestured to the chair opposite.

"Please."

She sat down, setting the folio on her knees. "I hope this isn't a bad time?"

It wasn't great.

"I can spare a few minutes." He lowered himself into his chair. "What can I help you with?"

She studied him with a direct, assessing gaze. "I'll get straight to the point, Sheriff, because I understand you had a significant incident last night, and I don't intend to take up more of your time than necessary."

She was well-informed.

"I received a formal complaint yesterday afternoon from Andre Caldwell. You may know the name?"

Savage wished he didn't, but he nodded. Andre Caldwell had come to town six months ago representing a Washington-based conglomerate that was proposing former ranch land be used to build a massive data center in the county. There had been a public outcry, both here and in Durango, but the proposal had gone before the council anyway. They'd yet to vote.

"The guy that proposed the data center," he said.

"Which he has every right to do. He is a legitimate stakeholder in the project." She opened the folio and took out a piece of paper.

"What is his complaint?" Savage didn't have time to argue the finer points of the proposal right now.

She set it down on the desk in front of him. "His site survey team was chased off municipal land at gunpoint yesterday morning by a woman named Clara McBride."

Savage resisted the urge to snort. Clara was a feisty landowner and long-standing citizen of Hawk's Landing. She and her forefathers had helped shape this county, and she was well-respected in the region. She was not the kind of woman who made idle gestures with a shotgun.

She also happened to be Deputy Lucas McBride's aunt.

Savage pressed a button on his desk phone. "Lucas, get in here," he said.

Monroe glanced at him in surprise.

"Family," he replied, nodding to Lucas as he walked in.

She nodded in understanding.

"What exactly did Caldwell say happened?" he asked, gesturing for Lucas to take a seat.

Lucas frowned, but sat on a vacant chair, his back to the window.

Monroe studied him, then turned back to Savage. "Caldwell's survey team arrived at the site, which is municipal land and therefore accessible under the terms of the planning application, and Ms. McBride approached them on horseback with a firearm and made clear they were not welcome."

Lucas folded his arms across his chest.

"Caldwell has lodged an official complaint and is requesting that appropriate action be taken. I'm not here to tell you what that action should be, Sheriff, as that's your domain. I'm here because I think you should hear this from me directly rather than through official channels."

"Appreciate it," he said with a grateful nod.

She was smart enough to know that he'd be acquainted with

Clara, or maybe she'd done her homework and realized his deputy was related. Either way, she was giving him a chance to talk to Clara before the situation escalated.

"I also think," she continued, closing the folio with a precise click, "that you should know I'm not unsympathetic to concerns about the data center proposal. My job is to make sure this council makes decisions based on sound process and with adequate information, and I intend to do exactly that." She stood, buttoning her coat. "But a woman pointing a shotgun at surveyors on public land is a problem I need you to address, regardless of the underlying merits of anyone's position."

"I'll speak to her," he promised, getting to his feet. Lucas did the same.

She nodded at them both, then left, leaving the complaint sheet on his desk. They heard her heels clicking across the office, then Barbara's voice as she let her out.

LUCAS TOOK Monroe's seat across from Savage and sighed. "Aunt Clara feels pretty strongly about the data center."

Savage dipped his head. "A lot of folks do."

They'd had plenty of protests over the last few months because of the proposal, and it was only getting worse. The further along they got in the process, the more intense they would get. Clara's reaction to the survey team was just one example of that.

"But shotguns aimed at survey teams are a different category of problem. You know that."

Lucas didn't argue, which Savage appreciated. Whatever his private feelings about his aunt's methods, Lucas understood the difference between family loyalty and professional obligation.

"You want me to talk to her?"

Savage gave a nod. "Yeah. She needs to understand that Caldwell now has a formal complaint on record, which means we can't ignore this. If she acts up again, we'll have to physically remove her from the site, and I don't want to have to arrest her."

That would really be poking the bear.

"I'll head out there now," Lucas said, turning to the door.

Savage nodded. "Thanks, but don't take too long. We need you back here to work on the case."

He gave a quick nod and left the office.

Savage picked up the phone to call Ray. He knew the autopsy had been scheduled for first thing that morning, and he couldn't wait for the official report.

FOUR

LUCAS DROVE the cruiser out to his aunt's ranch, which sat eight miles east of town on a parcel of land that had been in her family for two generations. Having been adopted by Clara's sister and her husband, a veterinarian from Buena Vista, he didn't identify with it the same way she did, but he had fond memories of the place.

A national forest bordered it to the north. It used to stretch into the foothills as far as the eye could see but was now crisscrossed by burn marks on account of the wildfires.

To the south was a long, shallow valley in which Hawk's Landing nestled. The access road was unpaved and rutted from the autumn rains, and Lucas's vehicle bucked and lurched along it with a rhythmic persistence that reminded him of Iraq.

Clara was in the yard when he pulled up, which meant she'd heard him coming a mile away, or seen the dust kicked up by his tires.

She was a lean, straight-backed woman in her mid-sixties, with close-cropped grey hair under a wide-brimmed hat and the kind of weathered face that came from decades of outdoor work in high-altitude sun. She carried a fence post and a mallet and showed no particular inclination to put either of them down.

"Hey, Aunt Clara," he said, getting out of the cruiser.

"I take it this isn't a social call?" she drawled, glancing at him from under her hat.

He tilted his head but couldn't resist a grin. "You know it's not."

"You here to arrest me?"

"You done something wrong?" he asked.

She sighed and set the fence post against the rail. "Those men had no business being out on that land."

"Actually, they did," he countered, leaning against the porch rail.

"The decision hasn't been made yet. Far from it," she complained. "The vote hasn't happened. How dare they walk around with survey equipment like they already own the place."

"They have to assess it to present to the council," he told her, even though she already knew that. She knew the process better than he did. Clara McBride had been part of this community all her life. He felt stupid having to explain it to her.

"That land has history," she said quietly. "Not that they care about that."

"What history?" he asked.

"The Garrity family owned that ranch back in the day. Gene and Lorraine and their two boys. Good people, proper ranching folk. They'd been there as long as we'd been here."

She paused, her gaze slanting toward the mountains.

"A development company approached them, oh, must be twenty years ago now. Wanted to buy them out for some kind of commercial project."

"What happened?"

"They refused."

At his surprised look, she nodded. "Oh, yes. These Washington bigwigs aren't the first ones to come sniffing around."

"But they did sell it," he said, frowning. "To the council."

"No, that's where you're wrong. They didn't sell."

He shook his head. "Then, what happened?"

"They died."

He stared at her. "Died? How?"

She adjusted her hat so it sat lower over her eyes. The sun wasn't particularly strong, but she did it anyway.

"There was a terrible fire. Nobody knows how it started. Happened at night while the family was asleep."

Lucas felt the dread rise in his stomach.

"Nobody made it out," she muttered, looking down at the ground.

Lucas cringed. Well, that put a different spin on things.

"Wasn't there an investigation?" he asked.

"The official report called it an accident," Clara continued. "Gas stove in the kitchen was deemed the source, but Gene Garrity was the most careful man I ever knew, and that ranch had a propane system that he maintained himself, every season without fail. I don't believe it was an accident, and I never will."

Lucas put his hands on his hips. "You think they were murdered?"

She fixed her gaze on him. "There's no way that man left the gas stove on."

He let out a long breath. "Those are some serious accusations, Aunt Clara."

"Just my opinion, that's all."

There was a short pause as he considered the implications of what she was saying.

"Who do you think was responsible? The development company?"

She shrugged. "Guess we'll never know."

He frowned. "What happened to the property?"

"Nothing. Commissioner Albright did what he could to keep any development off it. Said it was Gene's wishes, and he owed him that much. They'd been friends for years. And it worked, for a time." She looked out toward the mountain again. "Until now."

"I thought the council owned it?" he said.

"They bought it at auction," she said, her mouth flattening into a thin line. "Before anyone even knew it was up for sale."

"Is the Commissioner still around?" Lucas asked. It would be useful to get his side of the events. Maybe he'd be able to confirm what Clara had told him.

"Yeah, but he's not as active as he once was. Not sure he can hold them back this time. The same land that family died for is suddenly very attractive again."

She wasn't wrong there.

"Clara, I need you to stay off that land and away from Caldwell and his crew. Not because they're right and you're wrong, but because a formal complaint gives them leverage they didn't have before. You could get arrested over this if you don't quit bothering them."

Her hand clenched into a fist. "If we don't stop them, who will?"

"That's why there's a vote," he said, giving her a stern look. "It's not up to you. This is out of your control."

She huffed and picked up her mallet.

"Promise me you'll stay clear, Aunt Clara," he pushed.

She studied him, then gave a reluctant nod. "Okay, you've made your point. I'll leave 'em alone."

"Thank you," he said, relieved.

All he got in reply was a grunt as she turned toward the fence post again.

FIVE

SAVAGE PUT DOWN THE PHONE, drummed his fingers on the desk, then got to his feet. He walked into the main office and faced his team, all of whom looked up expectantly.

"Ray pulled two bullets from each victim," he said. "All four were intact, which is about the best forensic news we could have gotten given the absence of casings."

Savage glanced at Thorpe. "He suggested running the wound profile data through NIBIN."

The National Integrated Ballistic Information Network was a specialized computer network that contained digital images of recovered ballistic evidence.

Thorpe, the most technically minded of all of them, had come in midmorning after grabbing a few hours shut eye.

"Sure," he said with a nod. "I'll get right on it. Might help us identify if the firearm was used in previous incidents."

Savage turned to the whiteboard he'd set up against the far wall that morning. Frank and Sarah Wilson's names were printed at the top, their address beneath it, and not much else.

"What did you find out about the Wilsons?" he asked.

Sinclair looked up. "Frank Wilson was sixty-five, his wife Sarah was sixty-one. They have one grown son, Quentin, who lives in Virginia. I spoke to him this morning. He's flying in later today."

"Tell him to come straight to the Sheriff's office," Savage said.

"Already did."

"How'd he take the news?" Savage asked.

She shrugged. "As well as can be expected. He was upset, of course, and shocked by what had happened. Said he didn't know why anyone would want to harm his parents, let alone murder them."

Savage gave a nod. He'd find out more when he spoke to Quentin face to face.

"Also, they're both recently retired teachers from Black Rock High School." She glanced pointedly at Thorpe. "Isn't that where your girl Grace works?"

He swiveled away from his computer. "She does. Yeah."

"You think she knows them?" Savage asked.

"Maybe." Thorpe hesitated. "I could give her a call and find out."

"Ask her to come in, if she does," Savage said. "She might be able to provide some background information on the victims."

Thorpe reached for his phone.

"They were married for forty-three years," Sinclair said, almost wistfully. She glanced at the engagement ring on her finger. "I can't even imagine that."

Neither could Savage. He hadn't even managed one. Becca had called their engagement off when she'd left Hawk's Landing.

That's what happened when you didn't set a date, he thought sourly. He wished now he'd marched her down the aisle when he'd had the chance. Even pregnant with their son.

Or would it have just complicated their current situation?

He sighed. Didn't matter now.

"Motive," he said. "Let's focus on that. Why would the Wilsons be targeted? Let's talk to their friends and family. Try to trace their movements on their final days."

Everyone nodded except Thorpe, who held the phone away from his cheek. "Grace knew them well. She can come in during her lunch hour."

Savage gave him a thumbs up.

Thorpe turned back to the phone to confirm.

"Nothing was taken," Sinclair continued. "Pearl confirmed the house was undisturbed. Frank Wilson's wallet was still in his jacket pocket, her jewelry was on the dressing table. I think that rules out robbery, just in case we were still thinking along those lines."

"What about a personal grudge?" Savage asked.

Lucas, who had come back from Clara's ranch an hour ago and was sitting with his long legs stretched out and his arms folded, shook his head slowly. "Neighbors all said the same thing. The Wilsons were well-liked, no known disputes with anyone, no history of conflict. They were the kind of couple people waved at in the street."

"Debts? Financial trouble?" Savage rubbed his forehead.

"I've got a request in for their bank records," Thorpe said.

"Didn't look like they were in financial trouble," Sinclair pointed out. "The house was well-maintained, if a little old-fashioned. I didn't think it looked like they were struggling."

Savage grunted in agreement.

"Where does that leave us, then?" he asked.

"Maybe they witnessed something," Sinclair shrugged her shoulders. "Saw something they weren't supposed to."

It was possible.

"Must have been something serious to warrant a hit-style execution using military-grade equipment," Lucas pointed out.

The room was quiet for a moment.

"There must be something," Savage said, running a hand through his hair. "Couples like that don't just get taken out for no reason."

They were retired schoolteachers who had lived on Maple Ridge Lane for thirty years, who belonged to a book club and maintained their garden and left a bowl of candy out for trick-or-treaters. Yet someone with professional training and equipment had broken in on Halloween night and shot them both in cold blood.

"There is one thing," Lucas said, staring at his computer. "But it's probably nothing."

"Yeah?" Savage asked, pushing himself off Sinclair's desk.

"Frank Wilson volunteered at a community center out on Route 9, past the fairgrounds. According to their website, he helped retrain servicemen transitioning out of the military."

"Was Frank in the armed forces?" Savage frowned.

"No, neither of them were," Lucas confirmed. "They'd been schoolteachers their entire working lives."

Savage turned back to the whiteboard and stared at the two names written there. The blankness beneath them felt less like a lack of information and more like a deliberate absence, as if whoever had made the Wilsons a target had been determined not to leave a trace.

GRACE CALHOUN WAS a slight woman in her mid-thirties with pale blonde hair tied back in a neat bun. Savage had first met her when she'd been harassed by an obsessive ex-boyfriend against whom she had a restraining order. Thorpe had been assigned to her protective detail, after which they'd begun a romantic relationship.

Grace had also bravely offered herself as bait to help them catch a violent copycat killer even though she'd been terrified at the time. He admired her for that.

Usually prim and composed, she was anything but today. Her eyes were red and swollen, her bun messy, and it was obvious she'd spent the better part of the morning crying.

Thorpe was on his feet before she'd taken two steps inside.

"Hey," he said, quietly, going to her. "Hey, come here."

She pressed her face briefly into his shoulder, then pulled back and shook her head, attempting to hold herself together.

"Sorry," she sniffed. "I haven't been able to stop thinking about what happened. How is this even possible? Frank and Sarah were such decent people."

Nobody had an answer for that one.

Thorpe pulled up a vacant chair and led her to it. "Take a seat. Would you like something to drink? Some water?"

She shook her head.

Just as well, since the coffee machine still wasn't working.

"Did you know them well?" Savage asked, this time perching on Thorpe's desk.

"Yes, ever since I've been working at the school. They retired a few years ago, but they still came in from time to time. Sarah helped with the reading program, and Frank came to the reunions. The students and all the staff loved them." She shook her head, fresh tears running down her face. "I don't understand why anyone would want to hurt them."

"That's what we're trying to establish," Savage said. "Grace, I'm sorry to have to ask you this, but can you think of anything, anything at all, that might have made them a target? Anyone who had a problem with them? Anything they might have been involved in that felt out of the ordinary?"

Grace thought for a moment, then gave a helpless shrug.

"I really can't. I mean I didn't know them outside of school, but they always struck me as kind, law-abiding citizens. Frank volunteered at the community center, I think. Sarah was in a book club, and I think she also played bridge."

He nodded to Sinclair, who wrote a few notes on the crime board.

On the surface, they appeared to be good, decent people and active members of the community. It would require some deeper digging to figure out why they'd been targeted.

"Thank you, Grace," he said. "If you think of anything else, call us."

She nodded and stood up. “Sorry I couldn’t be of more help.”

Thorpe walked her out, while Savage stood up and stretched his neck. He needed some air and time to think.

“I’m going to visit the community center,” he was digging into his pocket for his keys. “You guys keep looking into the Wilsons. There’s got to be something we’re missing.”

SIX

BEFORE HE LEFT, Savage stopped by Lucas's desk. Earlier, his deputy had updated him on Clara McBride's claim that the Garrity family had been murdered for their land. Land that had never been sold to developers anyway, thanks to the efforts of Commissioner Albright.

The claim had stuck with him, blending with everything else he had going on in his head. Councilwoman Nancy Monroe's visit, the official complaint, the proposed data center, and most importantly, the double murder.

"When you have time, why don't you look into the fire at the Garrity place?"

"That was twenty years ago," Lucas pointed out.

"I know, but something about that doesn't feel right. See what you can find. Pull whatever records exist. There must be an official report somewhere."

Lucas nodded.

Savage thought for a moment. "Also, see if you can find out who owned the land between the Garrity family dying and the council acquiring it at auction. Clara said it went up for sale before anyone knew it was on the market."

Lucas arched an eyebrow. "Is this to do with the data center proposals?"

"I don't know. I just thought it might be worth looking into, that's all. Could be nothing."

His deputy nodded. "Sure. I'll see what I can find."

"Thanks."

It may have been before his time, but this was still his county, and Clara wasn't one to make up stuff like that. If she thought there was something shady about the fire, then he believed her.

Barbara glanced up as Savage walked past her desk. "Did I hear you mention the fire at the Garrity place?"

"Yeah. Clara McBride was talking about it. You remember it?"

Her expression hardened. "Of course I remember it. I think the whole town remembers it. That entire family was wiped out, even the two little boys. It was a tragedy."

"Clara seems to think there was something suspicious about it."

She sat up straighter. "Oh, I don't know about that. It happened at night, as I recall. There were rumors that Gene had left the gas stove on."

"You think that's possible?"

"Sure. I mean, gas stoves are dangerous, that's why they're installing electric ones nowadays." She shook her head. "They were well-liked, the Garritys. Proper old-fashioned ranching family and staunch members of the community."

"Do you know what happened to their land after they died?" he asked.

She pursed her lips. "Not sure. I know the council bought it, but I think that's because it fell to a distant relative who didn't want it. I'm not sure who."

"All right." Thorpe would find out. "Thanks, Barb."

The Hawk's Landing Adult Community Center sat on Route 9

heading out of town. A low, functional structure set back from the road behind a gravel parking lot. It wasn't the most impressive of buildings, but it did serve an important purpose.

Even from where he parked, Savage could see there were many sections to the sprawling prefabs. Some looked like windowed classrooms, while other, larger areas could have been halls or communal spaces.

Becca had done some therapy work here while she'd been on maternity leave, and he knew they offered job placement and skills retraining, along with counseling programs and veterans' support.

He got out of his truck and walked to the front entrance. Through the glass front door, he could see a reception desk and a corridor with noticeboards along the walls.

"Afternoon," he entered and nodded to the woman at the desk. "I'm Sheriff Savage from Hawk's Landing. Mind if I ask you some questions about Frank Wilson? I believe he volunteered here."

Her eyes widened, then immediately softened with grief.

"Of course, Sheriff," she said. Then, more softly, "We were devastated to hear about Frank and Sarah. What a terrible shock. Shot to death like that? It's almost unbelievable."

"You knew Frank well?" he asked.

"Ever since he started volunteering at the Veterans' Center," she said with a nod. "He was a math teacher, you see, so he helped retrain vets for job placements. We'll miss him."

Savage nodded. It was the same everywhere they went. The Wilsons were well liked, friendly, and engaged. Except someone had wanted them silenced.

"When was his class?" he asked.

"He volunteered every Tuesday and Thursday for the past four years. Such a patient man."

Savage frowned. "So there wasn't any tension with anyone in his classes? Difficult participants, anyone with PTSD or violent tendencies?"

"Heavens, no. Frank was a sweetheart. Many of our veterans are active members of the workforce now thanks to his efforts. They all liked and trusted him." She pointed over his shoulder. "That's him with some of our veterans at last year's spring barbeque."

He turned and studied the noticeboard, finding a photograph of Frank Wilson with a group of men. They stood outdoors, tall trees behind them, the sun shining on their faces. It was a wholesome, happy scene.

"Sheriff, is that you?"

He swung around to see Commissioner Albright walking down the corridor with a cane. Late sixties, heavyset, with the kind of silver-haired, broad-shouldered presence that had served him well over the years.

Savage had known him since the Frost Killer case, in which Albright's son's fiancé, Stephanie Harcourt, had been among the victims. He appeared frailer than Savage remembered, like he'd aged since then. But that was to be expected given the tragedy the family had suffered.

Albright had served in government for decades before he'd come home to run for office. Defense, intelligence—Savage had never quite worked out which alphabet had paid the man's salary, only that the connections he'd made there still ran deep.

"Commissioner," Savage said, shaking his hand. "I didn't know you were connected to this place."

"Board member," Albright said, with a modest inclination of his head. "Have been for years. I assume you're here about Frank Wilson."

Savage raised an eyebrow. "You knew him?"

"Oh, yes. Frank was one of our finest volunteers. His death is a real loss to the center." Savage saw genuine grief in the man's eyes. "Terrible business. Do you have any idea who was responsible?"

"We're working on it," Savage defaulted to his standard response when there wasn't anything to share. Not that he'd discuss an open investigation with a member of the public anyway, even if he was on the city council.

Albright gave a knowing nod, and they stood for a moment in the corridor, the photograph of Frank Wilson on the board between them.

"We had a formal complaint issued against Clara McBride the other day," Savage said, deciding it was the best way to bring up the land issue.

"Oh, yes?" He gave a reluctant grin. "What's that fine woman done now?"

"She threatened the surveyors off public land. With a shotgun. You know, the land that used to belong to the Garrity?"

Albright's gaze narrowed. "She did what now?"

"Yeah, and Andre Caldwell lodged a complaint. I got a visit from Nancy Monroe asking me to handle it."

Albright let out a low whistle. "She's got guts, old Clara. I know better than to mess with her."

"Still, she was out of line."

Albright didn't respond.

"I heard you had a hand in protecting the Garrity land after they died," Savage said.

Albright adjusted his hand on his cane. "That was a long time ago, Dalton. Why are you bringing it up now?"

"Same land Caldwell is after," he said with a shrug. "Thought you might have an opinion on that."

There was a long beat.

Eventually, Albright shook his head.

"Can't halt progress," he said with a sigh. "I managed to stop the developers back then by persuading the town council to bid for it, but now it's fair game. I have no say over what the council does with it."

"So, the town council bought it from the family?" Savage asked.

"Twenty years ago, yes. It went up for auction, and I and other interested parties convinced the council to buy it, either to develop it at some stage in the future, or to protect it, whatever the case may be. I was just glad it hadn't been turned into a luxury housing complex and golf course."

Interested parties being the Guardians, no doubt. The local, but powerful secret organization of landowners and influential townsfolk had a lot of sway back then. But Savage didn't say as much.

"And now they're considering selling it to the Washington conglomerate for a data center." Savage managed to keep his voice even.

"There is a lot of money involved, Dalton, and God knows this town needs it. That fire in the summer wiped out most of our crops and grazing land. The farmers are starving. The infrastructure needs rebuilding. The data center will bring much-needed jobs." He shrugged. "I know it's a goddamn eyesore, but what can you do? Maybe in this case, the benefits outweigh the inconvenience."

Savage drew in a breath. The Commissioner might have a point there, not that he wanted to admit it.

"I'll let you get on," Savage said, extending his hand.

"Good to see you, Dalton," Albright shook, then walked out into the late afternoon sunshine, his cane tapping along the asphalt to where his SUV was parked.

BACK AT THE sheriff's department, the team had been hard at work. Savage stopped in front of the crime board and assessed the new information. The Community Center link had been added, along with Sarah's book club and bridge club connection. Their son's name was there, and his address in Arlington, as well as his occupation as a software engineer.

"What kind of software engineer?" he asked nobody in particular.

"Defense," Sinclair responded, both eyebrows arched.

He paused. "Now that is interesting."

"That's what I thought," she said. "You think there's a connection with his parents' murders?"

"It's possible, I guess. Although I'm not sure why the hitman didn't target him, if that's the case."

"Maybe it was meant as a warning," Lucas suggested.

Savage gave a slow nod. "Do we know what kind of defense systems he's engineering?"

Sinclair looked back at her screen. "Doesn't say on his LinkedIn profile, and I can't find anything about it on his socials. He's pretty tight-lipped about his job."

Savage nodded. "When does he get here?"

"An hour or so. You can ask him all about it then."

He planned to.

"Hey, boss. I think I might have something here." Thorpe glanced up from his computer. His eyes were bloodshot behind his glasses.

"What've you got?"

Savage walked over to his desk.

"I've been running those bullets we recovered through various databases, and we've got a hit."

"You have?" He peered over his deputy's shoulder.

"It's not just the bullets, but the combination of the type of bullet, the double-tap pattern, and the placement of the wounds."

"Double taps are pretty common in military units," Lucas pointed out.

"But not always submandibular and temple," Thorpe said, nodding to his screen. "It appears the exact same weapon, placing and pattern were found in a couple of cases from twenty years ago."

"Twenty years?" Savage frowned.

"That's when the Garritys died in the fire on their property," Lucas said, putting his elbows on his desk.

"It's weird, though," Thorpe continued. "The cases have special operations classifications and are heavily redacted. I can't find out much about them other than the locations of the shootings."

"Where were they?" Savage's frown deepened.

Thorpe pushed his glasses up. "The hit locations were Istanbul, northern Iraq, and Cyprus. Three confirmed instances of the same method across a period of about eighteen months, all targeting individuals whose identities are completely blacked out in the records."

Savage exhaled, while both Lucas and Sinclair stared at him.

"Special ops missions," Sinclair murmured, running a hand over her hair. "What the hell were those two up to?"

SEVEN

THERE WAS A STUNNED SILENCE.

Savage spoke first. "You're telling me these were government sanctioned operations?"

"Looks like it," Thorpe shrugged. "But we won't know for sure until we have more information. From what I can see here, most of it is redacted and I don't have clearance."

Savage squinted at his deputy's screen. He saw the thick black lines over the text and the gaps in the report.

"Does that mean the same hit squad took out Frank and Sarah Wilson?" Sinclair asked, looking from Thorpe to Savage, and then to Lucas.

"That's ridiculous." Savage pointed at Thorpe's screen. "This was twenty years ago."

There was a long beat where nobody said anything. They were all pondering the likelihood of a two-decade old hit squad taking out a defenseless elderly couple.

"Have there been any similar incidents since then?" Savage asked, eventually.

Thorpe shook his head. "Nope. Cyprus was the last. Looks like the unit ceased operations after that."

"Can't be the same thing," Sinclair murmured, shaking her head.

"Still, the details match," Lucas said grimly. "If it's not a sanctioned op, then it's someone who was in that squad twenty years ago and hasn't forgotten how to kill."

A chill descended over the office.

"There's an assassin in Hawk's Landing?" Barb squeaked, coming to a halt in the middle of the room, yet another tray of coffees in her hands. Nobody made a move to grab any this time.

Was there? Was this even possible?

Shaking his head, Savage strode over and took the tray from her.

"Before we jump to conclusions, we need to find out more about this military hit squad," he said. "What type of ops were they involved in back then? Who was in it? I want names." He nodded to Thorpe as he set the coffee tray on his desk. "I don't care what you have to do to get them, but if there is the slightest chance that a member of that unit is in my county, I want to know who they are."

Thorpe gave a tight nod and turned back to his computer.

"What are you going to do?" Sinclair asked as Savage felt in his pocket for his keys.

"I'm going to speak to Zebediah Swift. He knew some guys in the military around that time. I'm hoping he'll know how we can get some answers."

THE HIDDEN GEM trailer park sat off the interstate, also known locally as Durango Road, behind a stand of cottonwoods that had turned a pale, washed-out gold in the November chill.

Savage pulled in just after four, the gravel crunching under his tires, and parked beside Zeb's Harley-Davidson motorcycle. Lights were on in the main mobile home. From somewhere behind it, he could hear a television and low voices, the usual quiet commerce of

Zeb's backyard trailers, which Savage continued to know nothing about officially.

He knocked twice and waited.

A moment later, a barefoot Zeb opened the door.

"Hey, Dalton. Didn't expect to see you."

"Who did you expect?" Savage asked.

He smirked. "Wouldn't you like to know."

There was laughter from out back. "Not interrupting anything, am I?"

"Nothing that can't wait. Come on in. You want a beer?"

"I'm good."

Zeb shrugged.

Zebediah Swift was only in his late forties, but he'd retired from the Force after an Internal Affairs investigation into ten kilos of cocaine that mysteriously went missing from a police evidence locker.

That was a while back now, but Zeb hadn't lost his instinct for trouble.

He knew everything that went down in this trailer park, and in the Crimson Angels MC, of which he was a "recreational" member—his words. Savage knew there was no such thing. You were either in or out. No in between.

Savage's theory was that he was the Angel's unofficial police advisor. He knew how cops thought, and therefore how best to avoid the law. Something the President, Rosalie Weston, would find very useful.

Zeb wasn't all bad, though. He'd saved Savage's life at least twice, and Becca's once, when he'd rallied the motorcycle club as backup. He still had those cop instincts, and every now and then, he proved useful.

"You heard about the double homicide in town?" Savage asked, following him into a comfy living area. Zeb sank into an armchair and gestured for Savage to do the same.

"Hard not to," he replied, as Savage sat down. "People are saying it was a professional hit."

"What people?" he asked.

"Is it?" Zeb pushed, avoiding the question. Savage knew he'd never give him names. Snitching was not something the ex-cop would ever do. Hence the reason Rosalie allowed him in the club.

"Looks like it, yeah." Savage hesitated. "We pulled up some similar hits back in the early 2000s. Same MO. Seems to be connected to a special ops unit although the details are a little hazy."

Zeb put down his beer. "Special ops? You thinking military?"

"I don't know. Was hoping you could help me with that." Zeb had served for two years prior to joining the police force.

"What's the MO?" Zeb asked, leaning back and eyeing Savage.

"Double tap, through the submandibular and temple." He gestured with his finger. "Identical in both victims. No casings."

"You think there was a casing capture system on the weapon?"

Savage gave a nod. "Bullets were embedded. We retrieved all four."

"That's how you got the match to the spec ops team?" Zeb asked.

"Yep."

Zeb was quiet for a moment, turning the bottle slowly in his hands.

"There was talk of an off-book outfit," he said, after a long moment had passed. "Totally deniable, of course. Ran for a few years in the early two-thousands, the Iraq and Afghan era, then got shut down after some fuck-up. I'm not sure what."

"How do you know this?" Savage asked, frowning.

"Fireside chatter," he said vaguely. "I don't know what the unit was called or who ran it." He paused and scratched his jaw. "But I know someone who might."

"Who?" Savage leaned forward.

"An intelligence agent with the Agency. Retired now but used to be based out of Denver. He was looking into them at one point. This was after I joined the Force."

"How'd you know him?" Savage wondered at the connection.

"Our paths crossed a few times." He shrugged. "Might even be dead now. He was pretty close to retirement back then."

"What makes you think he'd know about this unit?" Savage asked.

"He'd been asking questions. Seems there was some kind of internal investigation into the unit. That was before they disbanded."

"You got a name?"

Zeb gave him a hard look, then nodded. "Edgar Zales."

EIGHT

LUCAS FOUND Mason O'Riley at Fire Station One on Creekside Drive, where he was running equipment checks with two of his crew in the bay. The big overhead doors were open to the cold morning air, and the smell of diesel and clean hose rubber drifted out onto the street.

O'Riley crouched beside one of the engines with a clipboard, sleeves rolled to the elbows, despite the temperature.

He looked up when Lucas came in and raised a hand in greeting.

"McBride. Give me two minutes."

Lucas waited, watching the crew work. He'd gotten to know O'Riley well during the wildfire response in the summer. Working the lines together had a way of cutting through the small talk faster than anything else, and he liked him. Straight-shooter, competent, didn't waste words. He could see why Sinclair had gone for him.

O'Riley signed off on the clipboard, handed it to one of his crew, and walked over, wiping his hands on a rag. "Everything okay with Becky?"

"She's fine. This is about something else."

"Oh?"

Lucas frowned. "I'm looking into a fatal ranch fire that happened about twenty years ago. A family of four lost their lives in it. You know anything about that?"

O'Riley tucked the rag into his back pocket. "I heard about that. The old-timers talk about the bad ones. Garrity place, wasn't it?"

Lucas nodded. "That's right."

"Before my time. I hadn't even joined the service then."

"I read the official report," Lucas said, frowning. "They called it cut-and-dry and ruled it accidental."

O'Riley was quiet for a moment. "And you don't think that's the case?"

"I don't know. My aunt seems to think it was deliberate. The sheriff asked me to look into it."

"I know someone you can talk to. Max Hogarth. He was chief here for close to thirty years before he retired." Riley leaned back against the engine housing, his arms folded. "He's got a place out on Forest Road 14, past the Ridgeline turnoff, maybe twelve miles out. Old hunting cabin he fixed up when he retired." O'Riley tilted his head. "Thing is, he moves around a lot. Got kids scattered across three or four states, and he goes between them. Could be there, could be gone for a while."

"I'll give him a call before I head out there."

O'Riley gave a friendly nod, then pushed off the engine. "Tell him I sent you."

THE FIRST THING Lucas did when he got back to the department was search for a number for Max Hogarth. He found two. A landline and a cell. The landline was out of service. Hogarth had probably let it go since he didn't use it anymore. Not many people did these days. Times were tough, so why pay two bills when you only needed to pay one?

He tried the cell, but it just went to voicemail. An automated voicemail. Lucas debated leaving a message then decided against it.

He'd call back later. Or better yet, track him down in person and talk face to face.

He told Barbara where he was going, then set off for the forested area where Hogarth supposedly lived. The drive took the better part of forty minutes, and even when he got there, he wasn't sure he was in the right place.

The road O'Riley had mentioned wasn't even on a map. It was a service access road that led to a hiking trail deep in the national forest. It was narrow and gravely and he didn't want to think what it was doing to his suspension.

Eventually, he came to a clearing where the road ended. At the far side, away from the tree line, stood a large cabin.

Lucas slowed to a stop, engine idling for a moment before he cut it. He sat there briefly, taking it in. The cabin was impressively constructed, with thick, squared timber, darkened by years of exposure. It looked sturdy and warm, built to withstand the elements. The roof was pitched, presumably to shed snow, but the angle was steeper than most. A stone chimney rose along one side, broad and practical, built for draw and longevity rather than charm.

He got out of the cruiser and approached the cabin. The front porch was wide but bare, its boards clean and worn smooth by years of use. The posts were reinforced with iron brackets. A stack of split firewood stood to one side, cut to uniform length and half-covered against the elements with a tarp tied down tight against the wind.

Judging by the dust on the top, the covering hadn't been moved in a few days.

Damn. Looked like Hogarth wasn't here.

Still, Lucas walked up to the front door and knocked, just to be sure. The sound carried in the quiet clearing, sharp against the timber.

There was no response.

He tried again, louder this time, listening between knocks for movement, for the shift of weight inside, but when all remained silent, he gave up.

Hogarth clearly wasn't home.

Peering through the windows didn't help, either. They were darkened with a faint tint and set deep into the walls, the glass reflecting the trees back at him. He couldn't see inside.

Before he left, Lucas did a slow lap of the cabin, boots crunching over gravel and pine needles, looking for signs of life. There was no generator hum. No movement. Nothing.

The rear was no more revealing than the front. The interior lay in shadow, just another sign there was nobody home. There was no vehicle parked around the back either. Hogarth supposedly drove an old, mud-splattered Ford F-150 Raptor. The kind of truck built for logging roads and backcountry terrain.

Road trip to meet one of his kids, maybe? It wasn't just a trip into town for supplies, given the uncrushed leaves at the end of the road and the dust on the tarp. Nothing here said recent activity.

Defeated, Lucas left his card wedged in the doorframe, where it wouldn't blow loose, then turned and drove back to town.

NINE

IT WAS after five when Savage left Zeb's place, but instead of going home, he headed back to the office to interview Quentin Wilson.

"He's in your office," Barb said when he arrived.

"Thanks. Hey, before you go, will you book me onto a flight to Denver? Tonight."

Barb arched an eyebrow but nodded.

"What's in Denver?" Sinclair asked, as he strode past.

"Tell you later. You coming?"

She got up and followed him in.

"Sorry to have kept you," Savage said to Quentin as he took a seat behind his desk. Sinclair chose the chair by the window. "Thanks for coming in."

Quentin nodded. He appeared to be in his early forties, though the strain around his eyes added a few more years, as did the salt-and-pepper hair, graying more rapidly around the temples.

He wore dark jeans and a charcoal button-down shirt, sleeves rolled neatly to the forearms. Rectangular glasses caught the light when he turned his head. He was tall, but his shoulders were hunched, as if he was more used to leaning over screens than standing upright.

"I know this is upsetting, but before my deputy takes you to identify your parents' bodies, I'd like to ask you a couple of questions."

"About what?" he asked, frowning.

"Well, since this is a murder investigation, we thought you might be able to help us with our inquiries."

Quentin's eyes widened in understanding, and he gave a nod. "I don't know what help I'll be, but sure."

Savage glanced down at his notepad as if composing his thoughts. "Do you know any reason why someone would want to hurt your folks?"

Quentin gave a hard shake of his head. "Of course not. Why do you ask that?"

"It was the manner in which they were shot. It seemed... excessive."

"You think they did something to warrant this?" Quentin frowned. The smartwatch on his wrist buzzed, and he tapped it dismissively.

"Not at all," Savage reassured him. "But we think the shooter may have had military training."

Quentin gawked at him. "Military?"

Savage nodded, keeping his gaze fixed on the man opposite.

"My parents were never in the military."

"But you were," Savage prompted.

Quentin hesitated. "Is that what this is about? Me?"

"You did one tour in 2010, and you now work for a defense contractor," Savage repeated the information Sinclair had given him.

Quentin's gaze narrowed. "That's not a secret. I was a former Army Engineer Officer, nothing special. I didn't see active duty. It was more of a support role. Besides, why is that relevant?"

Savage kept his tone conversational. "We were just wondering if your parents were targeted because of something you're working on."

Quentin didn't react other than to simply stare at Savage. "My parents didn't know what I was working on. We never discussed my work."

"Which is what, exactly?" Savage asked.

"Software development for missile systems," he said without hesitation. "I can't go into specifics, obviously, but that's the gist of it."

"Isn't that top secret stuff?" Sinclair asked.

He shrugged, glancing across at her. "I don't design the systems, just the software to operate them. I wouldn't call that top secret."

Savage could tell by the careful look behind Quentin's eyes that he was playing it down.

"How often did you see your folks?"

"Not as often as I should have, I'm ashamed to admit." He hung his head. "I haven't been back to visit in... oh, maybe four months."

Savage supposed that wasn't that long, especially considering he lived in Virginia.

"Did you speak to them on the phone?"

"Sure, every couple of weeks."

"When was the last time?" he pressed.

Quentin sighed. "I don't know. Maybe two weeks ago. I can't remember exactly."

"How did they sound then?"

"Fine. Normal. Like they always sounded."

"Take me through your last conversation," Savage requested.

Quentin grimaced as if to question if this was really necessary.

"I spoke to my dad, like I usually do. He updated me on all the practical stuff. Then my mother came on and asked how I was doing. Whether I'm taking care of myself. When I'm coming to visit. You know how it goes."

Savage didn't. His own parents had passed a long time ago. But he could imagine.

Sinclair nodded. Her folks were alive and well in Hawk's Landing.

"They say anything was troubling them? Any threats? Anything unusual?"

"Nothing like that. It was just a normal conversation."

Savage sighed and leaned back in his chair. "You understand where we're coming from with this? Your parents were gunned down for no apparent reason. The method screams military. And you work on missile systems for a defense contractor."

He let that settle for a moment, studying Quentin. To be fair, the engineer did seem to be considering what he'd said.

Eventually, the man scratched his head. "If they were killed because of my job, surely I would have been contacted by the killers? I mean, if it was a message, where's the demand? If it was a consequence of something, I don't know what that could be. Sheriff, I'm not important enough to be targeted."

"You haven't had any requests for information? Any demands or threats?"

"Nothing. I would tell you if I had."

Quentin seemed genuine and was clearly a smart guy. Savage shook his head. "Okay, then. Well, if that changes, you'll get in touch?"

"I will."

Savage got to his feet. "Thanks again for coming in. Deputy Sinclair will escort you to the hospital to ID your parents now."

Sinclair nodded and got to her feet. "This way, sir."

Quentin pushed himself out of his chair and adjusted his glasses. "I hope you find the people who did this, Sheriff. My parents were ordinary, gentle people who didn't deserve this."

Savage dipped his head. "I'm doing my best."

Quentin gave a quick nod and walked out after Sinclair.

Savage watched him go, trying to decide whether he believed him or not.

SAVAGE LOOKED through the window as the plane descended over Denver. He could see the Mile High City spread out below, a grid of flickering amber lights against the dark plain, the mountains invisible behind it in the night sky.

They touched down at Denver International just after nine.

He disembarked, took a cab into town, and checked into a Holiday Inn on Colfax that he'd stayed at twice before on department business and which had the virtues of being cheap and close to where he needed to be in the morning.

He messaged Barb from the room to confirm he'd landed safely, then laid on the bed with his jacket on and stared at the ceiling for a while, thinking about Quentin Wilson and his careful eyes and his missile software and the way he'd claimed he wasn't important enough to be of interest to anyone.

That could be true, or it could also be the most practiced deflection Savage had heard in a long time. He hadn't decided which yet.

Tomorrow, he'd hire a car and drive to Edgar Zales' place. Zales had been cautious on the phone and had not extended a warm invitation. But he hadn't said no either, which Savage was treating as a yes.

He yawned, his thoughts shifting from Quentin Wilson to a special ops squadron active twenty years ago. Government sanctioned or not, he hoped Zales would be able to tell him more about it.

By ten thirty, Savage was asleep.

EDGAR ZALES LIVED in a ground-floor apartment on a quiet block in Washington Park. Having lived in Denver for most of his life, bar the last few, Savage knew the city like the back of his hand. This was a solidly middle-class neighborhood close enough to downtown to be convenient, but far enough out to feel suburban.

It boasted tree-lined streets and brick bungalows, as well as low-rise apartment blocks that had been standing for decades and were well looked after. Zales was in one of those.

He found the building without difficulty, buzzed the intercom, and waited.

There was a long pause, during which he wondered if Zales was even home. Then, a gravelly voice said, "Who is it?"

"Sheriff Dalton Savage, La Plata County. I called yesterday."

Another pause, shorter this time. The door clicked open.

"You'd better come in."

Zales was in his mid-seventies, lean and slightly stooped, with an angular face and pale eyes that still held their sharpness. He turned away without saying hello and went back the way he'd come.

Savage hesitated, then followed.

Zales moved slowly but walked without support. Once in the lounge, he gestured to the couch, then eased himself into an armchair. A folded newspaper sat on the pedestal table beside it, along with an empty mug of what Savage assumed had been coffee.

Zales didn't offer him anything, just watched with a calm, assessing gaze as Savage sat down. "You were a little cryptic on the phone, Sheriff. I take it that was intentional?"

No flies on this guy.

Savage masked a grin. "Yes, sir. We've got a double homicide in my town that mirrored a unit operational a couple of decades ago. A mutual friend suggested I get in touch. Thought you might know more about it."

Zales sat quietly, his pale eyes fixed on Savage.

"Tell me about it," he said, after a beat.

"Two retired schoolteachers in Hawk's Landing, shot on Halloween night. Double tap, submandibular and temple, identical shots in both victims." He paused, but Zales didn't comment, so he carried on. "There were no casings found at the scene. We think there was some kind of casing capture system on the weapon. My deputy ran the ballistics profile and got hits on three classified cases from about twenty years ago. Istanbul, northern Iraq, Cyprus."

Zales still didn't reply. He simply listened, his hands on the arm rests either side of him, his head upright, brow furrowed.

"The operational classification on the database records suggested a deniable special operations unit," Savage went on, when it became clear Zales wanted more information. "Everything else was redacted."

Finally, Zales said, "Who gave you my name?"

"He wouldn't want me to say," Savage hedged, hoping he wouldn't have to reveal Zeb's name. As it turned out, he didn't.

"Given you're from southern Colorado, it must be Zebediah Swift."

"Can you help?" Savage asked instead of confirming the guess.

"I was looking into it, yeah." Zales petered off, as if composing his thoughts. "It was a long time ago now."

"Anything you have might help."

"Department Nine. That's what they called it, though it never appeared in any official record under that name—or any other."

Department Nine.

Savage frowned. It sounded ominous.

"It came about in 2002, ostensibly as a counter-terrorism asset. Deniable operators who could be deployed in environments where conventional military or federal presence would be diplomatically untenable."

"Like the Middle East?"

Zales gave a quick nod. "They were involved with the targeted elimination of individuals deemed a threat to national security interests. Terrorist leaders, enemy dictators, that kind of thing."

Savage nodded, hanging on to every word.

"Who ran it?"

Zales drew in a breath. "Officially, it didn't exist, so officially nobody ran it. It was handled through a private contractor with deep government connections. The Agency, principally, although State Department ran the diplomatic cover. It was funded through discretionary channels that were designed to be untraceable."

"How do you know this?"

Zales folded his hands in his lap.

"I spent three years trying to build a case against it after reports of civilian fatalities in southern Iraq. I got close enough that certain people became aware of my interest, and shortly after that, the unit stood down. I was told to cease the investigation."

"This was a CIA investigation?" Savage asked, just to be clear. He wanted to make sure Zales hadn't been on some vigilante quest.

Zales nodded. "Fully sanctioned by my department and requested after the botched Iraq operation."

"Do you know the names of anyone involved in this unit?"

"No, I don't." But the slightest hesitation gave him away.

Savage leaned forward. "Mr. Zales, two retired schoolteachers lost their lives this week for no apparent reason. If there is a member of Department Nine operating in Hawk's Landing, then I need to find out who it is and why he's targeting my citizens."

Zales studied him intently. "You really think it's one of them, after all this time?"

Savage shrugged. "The MO fits."

Zales pursed his lips as if trying to decide something. Slowly, he pushed himself out of his chair. "Wait here."

Savage waited as Zales walked out of the room. He heard the sound of boxes being shifted, followed by several grunts, and the sound of paper rustling. Then the old man was back. In his hand was a faded manilla folder. He dropped it in Savage's lap.

"Everything I have on them is in there."

Savage glanced down. The corners of the folder were curling with frequent use, there were ring stains on it from too many coffee cups, and a thumb print in blue ink.

"Thank you," he said, opening it to take a look inside. The pages were much the same. Zales had spent a lot of time on this case. "You sure you don't mind?"

He grunted. "Not a lot of good to me now."

Savage nodded. It would make good plane reading.

He got up, thanked Zales again, and tucked the folder under his arm.

"You want me to keep you updated?" he said, figuring it was the least he could do. The old guy had spent so much time on the investigation only to have it go nowhere.

Zales nodded. "Sure, why not?" He tried to appear like he didn't care either away, but Savage saw the glimmer of interest in his pale blue eyes.

"Okay, then."

He said goodbye and headed to the door. Zales didn't follow.

TEN

THE FLIGHT to Durango only took an hour, during which Savage devoured the contents of the folder. Zales had been thorough, documenting everything he'd discovered about Department Nine.

The first few pages contained fragmented background information, heavily inferred and pieced together from redacted reports, procurement trails, and partial testimonies. Names were absent, blacked out, or never written down in the first place.

Savage tried to piece it together.

Department Nine had been a small selective unit composed of operators pulled from special forces units, intelligence backgrounds, even private sector contractors. There was no obvious chain of command. No paper trail that led anywhere useful. Missions were greenlit through what Zales described as "discretionary authorizations," routed through intermediaries designed to insulate the people giving the orders.

Deniable, just like Zales had said.

Savage turned the page. The next section was different. Denser. The margins were filled with handwritten notes in a tighter, more urgent script.

INCIDENT: SOUTHERN IRAQ — AL-HADIR REGION — 2004

A grainy satellite image had been printed out and annotated. It showed a cluster of low-lying buildings in the middle of scrubland. A dirt track led in from the west. Zales had circled the compound in red ink.

PRE-STRIKE ASSESSMENT:

High-value insurgent cell believed to be operating from location. Confirmed via signals intercept and human intel.

Below that, another note, underlined twice:

SOURCE RELIABILITY?

Savage tightened his jaw and read on.

The operation had taken place just before dawn. The unit had been inserted overnight with the express purpose of close-range engagement. There were no apparent explosives or accompanying air support. It was to be a clean entry and controlled sweep of the premises with the goal to eliminate all occupants.

Savage didn't need to read the next line to know what was coming.

POST-STRIKE FINDINGS:

Targets not present.

Occupants: civilian. Multi-family residence.

He exhaled long and slow. It was worse than he'd imagined. Zales hadn't given him fair warning when he'd said civilian fuck-up.

Nine confirmed dead. Possibly more. Women. Children. An elderly couple. One male adult identified posthumously as an aid worker employed by a local program.

Savage's grip tightened on the page.

There were photographs clipped behind the report that he didn't want to look at. He made himself do it anyway. Black and white, low resolution, but clear enough. Bodies laid out in rows. They were covered with blankets. None of the faces visible.

Not wanting to linger, he flipped the page.

AFTER ACTION RESPONSE:

Local unrest. Militia presence reported within hours. Coalition forces denied involvement. The incident remained classified.

Below that in Zales's handwriting:

Intel was bad.

Savage kept reading. What followed was where it shifted from tragedy to something else entirely.

SECONDARY DEPLOYMENT (48 HRS POST-STRIKE)

He frowned as he stared at the page, trying to understand. The same unit had gone back in?

Officially, there was no record of it. Unofficially, Zales had reconstructed it from witness statements that had never made it into the formal reports. Interviews conducted off-book via sources that had later recanted or disappeared.

He took a sharp breath in. Probably survivors, but they'd been scared or injured, and not willing to talk.

He felt a cold weight settle in his chest as he read the next line.

OBJECTIVE: CONTAINMENT

Department Nine had returned to clean up the mess. To eliminate those who could testify. They'd protected themselves, or the people who had sent them in.

Zales's notes filled the margin. The ink was darker, pressing harder into the paper.

Witnesses eliminated. Site burned. No recoverable forensic evidence.

Savage stared at the words for a long moment before he turned to the next page. That was where Zales came in.

CIA INVOLVEMENT — INITIATED 2005

A formal request had been logged after conflicting intelligence reports had surfaced. Civilian casualty estimates didn't align with the official version of events.

Zales had been assigned as part of a small investigative team tasked with determining whether a covert U.S.-linked operation had resulted in unlawful civilian deaths.

At first, it had been routine. A box-ticking exercise. Then the anomalies started stacking up.

Intercepts that didn't match the timeline. Satellite imagery that had been altered. Field reports that had been amended after submission. And always, just at the edge of it, references to a unit that didn't exist.

Department Nine.

Savage read Zales's summary.

Initial resistance encountered at State Department level. Access to classified materials restricted without explanation. Two witnesses recanted statements under unknown circumstances. One source deceased prior to follow-up interview.

He let out a quiet breath.

They'd shut it down. The whole thing. Prevented the Agency from conducting an effective investigation. The State Department had protected the unit.

The final section was brief.

STATUS CHANGE — 2006

Department Nine stood down. Funding channels terminated. Contractor relationship dissolved. No explanation given.

Zales's last note sat alone at the bottom of the page.

Robert Carver, State Department. Told me the unit had been disbanded and to quit the investigation. Benjamin Vance, the Agency's senior man on the program, seconded the call. Case shelved.

The plane lost altitude as it began its descent. Savage was about to close the folder when a smaller piece of paper fell into his lap.

He picked it up and studied it. Hadn't seen that in the back. It was a handwritten list, in blue ink, faded with age. No heading. No introduction.

Eight names.

He read through them, then frowned. Were these the alleged operators? The members of the unit? And if so, how the hell had Zales gotten his hands on them?

Savage returned it to the folder and put the whole thing into his duffel bag. As he got off the plane, he couldn't help but wonder... After twenty years, was one of these men active again?

Had they targeted Frank and Sarah Wilson?

And then there was the overriding question:

Why?

ELEVEN

SAVAGE DROPPED his duffel bag on the floor and turned to face his team. He'd come straight from the airport, but for the first time since the double shooting, he finally felt like they had something to be going on with.

"Listen up," Savage said, as they swiveled to face him. Thorpe looked better rested today, and Sinclair and Lucas seemed fresh and ready to get down to work.

Even Barb came out of her enclosure to listen.

The coffee machine was still broken.

"I went up to Denver to speak to a retired CIA analyst, Edgar Zales. Zebediah Swift gave me his name. He headed up the Agency's investigation into the unit we're interested in."

"You found a link?" Thorpe asked.

"I did more than that." Savage held up the folder. "Zales gave me this. It contains everything he discovered on the black ops unit known as Department Nine."

"Department Nine," Sinclair murmured. "That sounds suitably vague."

He gave a nod. "It's interesting reading. Barb, I need you to make copies for everyone."

She nodded.

"Nothing on the servers," he cautioned. "This is For Your Eyes Only."

Nods all round.

Then, he walked them through Department Nine, the Iraq incident, the civilian deaths, and the clean-up operation.

"If it's true, it's shocking," Sinclair hissed under her breath.

"That's what brought it to the attention of the Agency," he told them.

"But nobody was ever held accountable?" Lucas asked, shoulders stiff.

"The unit was disbanded and the investigation shut down in 2006. Zales was told to drop it by a State Department agent by the name of Robert Carver. Let's look into him."

Lucas made a note of the name.

"I also found this." Savage held up the smaller sheet of paper. "It's a list of names that Zales inserted in the back of the folder. I suspect they belong to the men in the unit."

Lucas let out a low whistle. "How'd he get these?"

Savage shrugged. "I don't think I want to know. Knowing who these men are is dangerous. Zales kept it hidden all these years, so let's make sure we keep it that way. Unless, of course, one of these guys is running around our town shooting up our inhabitants," he added.

Thorpe held out a hand. "Can I take a look?"

"Barb first," he said, handing the folder to her. She hurried off to the copier. If any one of them spilled something on it, or tore it by accident, the names would be irretrievable.

"Thorpe, I need you to run every single one through whatever databases you have access to. Watch lists, federal systems, criminal databases, international wanted lists, the works. I want to know who's still active, who's dead, who's changed their name, and who's been anywhere near La Plata County in the last month."

"On it," he said, as Barb came back and handed out the photocopies, neatly stapled into three stacks. He turned to the last sheet and glanced down at the list. "I'll look for known associates and any aliases too."

"Whatever it takes."

THEY WORKED through the afternoon with an intensity rarely seen in the department. Barb fielded all phone calls and only transferred those that were emergencies. Radios were kept on low, the usual background chatter replaced with the soft clatter of keyboards and the occasional scrape of a chair.

Savage spent most of it in his office with the door open, checking possible names and aliases against local hotel reservations, motel logs, and inn bookings. He cross-referenced dates, ID numbers, anything that might flag a transient passing through under the radar.

Every so often he'd step out, get an update, and head back again.

Halfway through the afternoon, a brand-new coffee machine got delivered. Barb had ordered it from a local supplier and put a rush order on it. They'd paid more than they'd needed to, but he wasn't arguing. You couldn't put a price on some things.

She set it up on the side counter, filled the reservoir, ran it through its cycle, and within minutes the smell of freshly brewed coffee cut through the stale air, lifting all their spirits.

By late afternoon, the light had shifted and shadows reached across the office floor. Sighing, Savage stopped working and stretched his neck. He hadn't found anything worth the paper it was printed on.

Too many dead ends. Too many names that led nowhere.

He was staring at a list of reservations from a roadside motel, the names swimming in front of his eyes, when there was a knock on the doorframe.

"We got something, Sheriff," Thorpe said, rubbing his eyes beneath his glasses. He looked worse than Savage felt.

Glad of the break, he pushed up from his desk. "I'll come out."

He followed his deputy to his desk. The others had stopped working and everyone was poised, wondering what Thorpe had found.

"Okay. Shoot."

Thorpe stood in front of his computer and pointed to the screen. "Several of the names on that list are ghosts. No trace of them, no current records on any system."

"How d'you explain that?" Savage asked.

He frowned. "They could be dead, could be living under completely different identities. That's the most likely."

"What about the others?" Savage asked.

Thorpe nodded. "Three of the eight have criminal records under their given names. Low-level stuff, but nothing recent. We know where they're living and can easily check to see where they were the night of the murder."

"I'll get on that," Sinclair said.

"What about the last one?" Savage asked.

Thorpe pushed his glasses up with one finger. "That's the interesting part. The last name has a known alias that has recently been active."

The office went quiet.

"Who?" whispered Savage.

"Victor Gregory." Thorpe turned the monitor so they could all see. A grainy photo filled the screen, along with lines of data.

"There's a Europol watch list entry from 2009. Suspected involvement in two contract killings in Eastern Europe. Gregory was never charged. He went dark after that."

"That's not recent," Savage pointed out.

"No." Thorpe swiveled to face him. "But get this. One of Gregory's known aliases is Arthur Renner. An Arthur Renner checked into the Ridgewater Casino two days ago. And according to the hotel receptionist"—he glanced up at Savage—"he's still there."

THEY TOOK TWO VEHICLES, Savage driving the Suburban with Lucas beside him, and Sinclair following in her cruiser. They made the drive out to the Ridgewater Casino in under twenty minutes.

The casino sat on the southern edge of Ute land, a gleaming building set against the mesa, its signage lighting up the early evening haze.

The parking lot was half full of the mid-week crowd when Savage pulled in. Above the casino was the plush resort hotel, while behind, out of sight of the main entrance, were the sprawling staff quarters.

Savage leading the way, they strode inside where the noise hit them like a wall of sound. The pinging, beeping and jingling of the slot machines, the clatter of a roulette ball, the low murmur of the blackjack tables. It was a sudden and intense onslaught, made worse by the bright lighting and lack of windows, all designed to make you forget what time of day it was.

Lucas, who hadn't been there before, stalled to take it all in, until Sinclair gave him a nudge. "Come on, the administrative office is on the mezzanine floor."

With Savage leading the way, they took the escalator up one level and stopped at the reception desk.

"Sheriff Savage," he said, flashing his badge. "I need to see Sam Walking Deer."

Sam Walking Deer had been the casino manager since it opened a couple of years back. Savage knew him, and his head of security, Jonas Half Moon, from a previous case. Both men had proved helpful when a Denver mobster, who happened to be part-owner of the casino, had been utilizing the venue for his illegal betting racket.

The casino didn't have a spotless record, but they were trying to clean up their image and bring back the tourists. They wouldn't want to be seen harboring a double murderer.

At least, that's what Savage hoped.

As expected, Sam was compliant, summoning Jonas to escort them to Arthur Renner's room. It was on the fifth floor, accessible by an elevator and an emergency staircase.

The team split up.

Lucas took the stairs, then positioned himself at that end of the long corridor, while Savage and Sinclair accompanied Jonas in the elevator.

"Wait here," Savage told Sinclair, as he set off with Jonas along the corridor. They passed roughly ten rooms before coming to a corner.

Savage glanced up at the ceiling. "Doesn't look like you have any surveillance cameras along here."

Jonas shrugged. "We have one at the elevator, and one at the stairway."

"Do they cover the corridor?"

"To a certain extent. They're mostly for the elevator landing and stairwell."

Savage nodded. Room 514 was midway, the first door on the left after the corner. There was a Do Not Disturb sign hanging on the door.

They stopped outside it. There were muffled television sounds from inside.

"Sounds like he's inside," Savage muttered, drawing his weapon.

He nodded to Jonas, who knocked three times. "Hello? It's hotel security, Mr. Renner."

Silence.

He knocked again. "Mr. Renner, do you mind if we come in?"

Savage intended to announce himself, but only after Renner opened the door. He didn't want to spook the guy. But there was no movement. No sound other than the false laughter of a sitcom.

"Let's go in," he said to Jonas.

The head of security inserted a keycard and pushed the door open. Then he stood back to let Savage enter.

The stench reached him before his eyes had time to adjust to the dim light. It was that flat, coppery scent he'd encountered enough times in his career to recognize immediately.

"Shit," he muttered, stepping inside.

The curtains were drawn. He flicked a light switch and braced himself for what he was about to see.

Victor Gregory—the man who had checked in as Arthur Renner—sat in an armchair by the window, chin on his chest, resting in a position that might have suggested sleep if not for the bloodstains across his face and chest.

He'd been shot twice.

Savage didn't need to get close to see the placement. Submandibular and temple. Identical to the Wilsons.

TWELVE

"GET MY DEPUTIES IN HERE," Savage barked to a white-faced Sam Walking Deer, who'd come in behind Jonas Half Moon.

"Jesus. Is that—?"

Savage turned and waved him out.

"Oh, yeah. Sure." The hotel manager backed out, nearly tripping over a pair of jeans on the floor as he went.

Jonas didn't move. He just stood in the entrance, staring at the victim.

"This is now a crime scene, Jonas," Savage turned to face him. "I'm going to need you to call the Tribal Police. The res is their jurisdiction."

He had to play by the book, and he needed Jonas out of there so he could take some photographs before the case got taken out of his hands.

Sinclair rushed in as Jonas left, closely followed by Lucas. Both had their weapons drawn.

"Holy shit," she blurted when she saw the body. "Is that him?"

"Victor Gregory, yeah."

Lucas scratched his head. "I thought he was the killer."

"So did I." Savage gestured around the room. "Tomahawk is going to be here soon, so let's photograph everything. Get as many shots as you can. Once he arrives, this isn't our crime scene anymore. We've got ten minutes, maybe fifteen, tops."

The Southern Ute Tribal Police Department was less than three miles away. After the call came in from Jonas, they'd take a couple of minutes to mobilize and then they'd be on their way.

While his team worked the scene, Savage studied the victim. Heavyset, mid-forties, with close-cropped grey hair and a broad face that had probably been hard and watchful in life but was now simply still.

The television was on some kind of comedy show, the canned laughter incongruous in the dim room harboring a dead body. Savage left it running. Tomahawk had to see it as it was. As undisturbed as possible.

He peered behind the armchair but couldn't spot any exit holes. Both rounds were likely still inside the victim. He'd also bet good money they were the same type of bullets as before.

But how had the shooter gotten access?

They'd used the security manager's keycard to get in, and there had been no sign of forced entry.

Just to be safe, Savage went back and inspected the door. The locking mechanism was intact. Not a scratch on the door. Nothing had been forced. Plus, Gregory was seated in the armchair and hadn't fallen near the door, which suggested he hadn't been alarmed when the shooter came in.

Savage exhaled as he extrapolated. Either Gregory had opened the door himself, or the shooter had come in while he dozed in the armchair and surprised him. Either way, it had been quick and brutal, same as the Wilsons.

"Size eleven," Lucas said, holding up a boot. "There's also dirt in the grooves. Could match that from outside the Wilson's house."

"Take a sample," Savage said, glancing to the door to make sure nobody was watching. He knew it was risky, but it was unlikely

Tomahawk would try to match this footprint to the one outside the Wilsons. If he wanted a match, he'd have to do it.

"Hey, over here," Sinclair called. He went over to where she was standing by the bedside drawer and looked inside.

"A men's travel bag?"

"Wait." With gloved hands, she pried it open. Inside was a box of ammunition. Taking it out, she opened the box and held up one of the bullets.

Savage sucked in a breath. "They look like bonded duty rounds. Same as the ones used to murder the Wilsons."

"Looks like he's our killer," Lucas muttered, coming over.

"Should we take them into evidence?" Sinclair asked, slotting the bullet back in the box.

Savage hesitated. It would make life easier if they had an actual bullet to compare with the ones found in the Wilsons. Still, this wasn't his jurisdiction, and one less bullet would raise questions if this was ever linked to the double shooting.

He could justify the dirt, but not the bullet.

"No, leave them," he decided, ignoring her raised eyebrow. "This isn't our crime scene."

She nodded, put the bag back in the drawer, and closed it.

"I need to talk to Jonas," Savage said, heading for the door. "Let's clear out. Tomahawk is going to be irritated enough that we've been in here at all."

"Nearly done," Sinclair said, crouching in front of the body for some close-ups.

He stepped into the corridor and met Jonas, who was on his way back.

"He's on his way," he said, and glanced at the open door. "You guy's done?"

"Yeah. We'll leave that to the tribal police."

Jonas hesitated. "We haven't had a dead body at the casino since... well, since you were here last winter. And that was outside."

"I know it's a shock," Savage said. Jonas might be head of hotel security, but he was still a civilian. He didn't have a background in law enforcement or the military. "Tomahawk will be here soon, and he'll deal with it."

Jonas gave a relieved nod.

"Who has access to these rooms?" Savage asked.

"Apart from housekeeping, only the guests themselves."

"Was anyone cleaning today?"

"Housekeeping turns over the rooms every morning unless there's a Do Not Disturb on the door." Jonas nodded at where the sign was still hanging over the handle of room 514. "So they left it."

Which was exactly what the shooter had wanted. When Gregory failed to check out, hotel management would have entered the room. By then, the killer would have been long gone.

"When was he due to leave?" Savage asked.

"Tomorrow morning," Jonas said. "Eleven o'clock."

Heavy footsteps marched along the corridor. Savage looked up to see Tomahawk Winter approaching with two of his officers, a dour expression on his face.

"Sheriff," he said, offering Savage a nod.

"Tomahawk." Savage fell into step beside him.

"You found the body?" the police chief asked.

Savage nodded. "Victim is a suspect on a case I'm working. Or rather, he was."

Tomahawk frowned. "What made you come out here?"

"We saw he'd checked into the casino and came to talk to him." He gestured to the open door. "We found him like this."

Tomahawk stepped inside, then drew in a breath. The two officers who walked in behind him did the same. One covered their nose.

"It was a professional hit," Savage said, following them in. "Same MO as my investigation."

"Same killer?" Tomahawk asked, his gaze on the victim.

Savage shrugged. "Could be."

Given the box of ammunition they'd found in the drawer and the boot size, Savage was willing to bet Victor Gregory was their killer, but he didn't say as much. Explaining would take too long.

Tomahawk crouched in front of the victim, studied the wounds, then straightened. He waved his officers back into the corridor, then turned to face Savage.

"I'll have to bring in the Feds," he said. "We don't have the facilities for this."

Goddammit. Not the FBI. The moment they swooped in was the moment the sheriff's department would lose access to this case.

"We can take it," he said. "I've got an ME and a forensic expert on standby."

Tomahawk shook his head. "Wish I could, Dalton. But I've got to follow protocol. I could get into trouble if I hand this over to you."

"It's related to my investigation," he stressed.

"The body is on reservation land."

"The people who hired whoever that was," Savage said, nodding toward the armchair, "are in my county. The other victims live in my county. I'm not walking away from this."

Tomahawk looked at him for a long moment. "I will talk to the Feds when they arrive, tell them you have a related investigation. Beyond that, it's out of my hands."

Like that would help.

He sighed. "Can we at least look at the surveillance footage?"

Tomahawk hesitated, then gave a curt nod. "Sure, but I lead."

Jonas led them to the security suite situated on the ground floor. It was a compact room lined with monitors showing feeds from across the resort. The gaming floor with its rows of slot machines and green-felt tables, the lobby with its plush carpeting and warm lighting, the front entrance, the parking lot, and several corridor feeds covering the main access points of the hotel.

The operator pulled up the footage for the fifth-floor corridor at Tomahawk's request.

"I thought you said it covered the corridor," Savage said, grimacing.

“I said it covered part of it,” Jonas said, a touch defensively.

“A small part,” Savage muttered. The downward angle of both surveillance cameras meant they covered the elevator landing and the top of the stairs beyond a security door, and about three or four yards down the corridor, but no further than that.

“We can’t see who went into that room?” Tomahawk asked.

“No,” Jonas said. “We can see who comes out of the elevator or uses the emergency staircase. We don’t put cameras in the corridors themselves, as a privacy consideration for our guests.”

“Okay,” Savage said, shelving his disappointment. If that’s all they had, they’d have to work with it. “Let’s go back to six p.m. the night he checked in, on the elevator feed.”

The operator did as he asked, then ran the footage at speed, slowing to real time whenever a figure appeared on the landing.

The first guest to appear, at seven thirty-five on the footage, was a hunched, elderly man with a walking stick moving slowly across the landing before disappearing from view down the corridor.

“Not sure which room he’s in,” Jonas said. “There are only six occupied on this floor. I’ll have to go down to reception and check his ID against the booking on the system.”

“We’re going to need a list,” Tomahawk said.

The next time he slowed the footage was when a young woman in a short skirt, leather jacket and heels entered the frame. She exited the elevator just after eleven thirty and walked down the corridor out of the camera’s line of sight.

Jonas gestured to the screen. “Victoria Davis. She’s in 508.”

“How do you know?” Tomahawk asked.

“Helped her carry her suitcase up to the room,” he replied.

Savage noted it down. “You often help the guests?”

He shrugged. “I was passing and she needed a hand. I’m a nice guy. What can I say?”

“Who’s that?” Tomahawk asked, pointing to a different screen where a Native American man had appeared. “That’s the camera at the top of the stairwell, right?”

Jonas nodded. "Yeah. Most people take the elevator."

"Maybe he didn't want to be seen," Savage muttered, studying the guy. He had long hair tied back in a low ponytail and wore leather trousers and a denim jacket over a white T-shirt. They watched as he stepped through the security door at the top of the stairs, then hurried down the corridor, out of sight.

Savage checked the timestamp. Eleven fifty.

"He's not armed," Tomahawk said.

"We don't know that," Jonas replied. "Could be carrying concealed."

Savage gave a small nod. It was possible. There were plenty of ways to hide a weapon. Still, it didn't fit. Not with the caliber used in the shooting. Whoever pulled the trigger had almost certainly used a suppressor, and there was no way that guy was carrying all that hardware.

"Let's move on," Savage said.

A man in a business suit stepped out of the elevator next. The timestamp was close to midnight. He walked out of frame, then reappeared a minute later, lingering near the elevator as if undecided. After a moment, he turned and headed back down the corridor.

"Doesn't know what he's doing," Tomahawk muttered.

"Or maybe he does," Savage said, gaze narrowed. "Who is he?"

Jonas shook his head. "I'll need to check."

"Wait." Savage pointed. "That's him again." Nearly three hours had passed on the footage, but only seconds for them.

The man was moving faster now. He kept close to the wall as the elevator opened, stepped inside quickly, then took position at the back, out of sight from anyone in the hall.

Savage leaned forward, reading the timestamp. Twenty-three minutes past two in the morning.

"I need to know who that man is," he said.

Jonas didn't respond, but he kept the footage running.

At half past two, a young man—late twenties—strolled out of

the elevator, hands in his pockets, yawning as he went. He stopped at the first room on the landing, well within the camera's view, and used a keycard to let himself in.

Savage watched the door close. He'd been on camera the whole time.

Shortly after, a well-dressed woman came into view, her blouse askew, hair loose. She clung to a man's arm, laughing, both of them unsteady.

Much later, at 04:42 a.m., a rotund man in his late forties stepped out of the elevator. He had the pale, soft look of someone who spent most of his life sitting down. Savage pegged him as a career gambler.

All four appearances came after two in the morning.

Without a confirmed time of death, Savage couldn't be sure any of them mattered, but he noted descriptions and timestamps anyway and asked Jonas to pull registration details.

He was about to call it when the man who'd earlier been propping up the laughing woman came back into frame. He wasn't laughing now. His stride was tight, hurried. He kept his head down, jaw set, like he didn't want to be recognized. Same pattern as the businessman, fast to the elevator, impatient as he waited.

Savage leaned in, catching the timestamp. 06:15 a.m.

"Walk of shame?" Jonas muttered.

Savage didn't answer. Something about it didn't fit. The woman had barely been steady on her feet. He'd been holding her up then. Now he looked like he wanted out before anyone saw him.

"He went up after two," Tomahawk said. "Not sure he's our guy."

"Still, I'm going to need all their names," Savage said, glancing at Jonas.

Jonas didn't respond straight away. He looked to Tomahawk instead. A brief pause, then Tomahawk gave a small nod.

"We'll see what we can do," he said.

Savage had to be content with that.

THIRTEEN

SAVAGE HADN'T REALLY SLEPT.

He'd closed his eyes for a few hours, maybe, but his mind had kept turning, dragging him back through it all in fragments that didn't quite line up. Faces. Names. Loose ends.

The Wilsons. Edgar Zale. Victor Gregory. The video surveillance at Ridgewater Casino.

It circled without settling, like something just out of reach. There was a connection—there had to be—but every time he thought he was close, it slipped away again.

Sometime in the early hours, he'd given up on sleep altogether.

To make matters worse, when he'd gotten home from the crime scene at the casino, he'd tried to call Becca—just to hear her voice. But she hadn't picked up. Probably too late by then, but he'd been hoping to catch a glimpse of his son. He'd needed the connection to something real, something pure and innocent, to ground him. To take him away from all the death and confusion.

By the time the first light started pushing at the edges of the sky, he was already dressed. Already moving. The night hadn't resolved anything. It had just left him with more questions.

The sheriff's department was still mostly dark when he let himself in, the place quiet around him. Rubbing his eyes, he walked over to the shiny, new coffee machine. At least he could make himself a decent cup of coffee.

Armed with caffeine, he stepped into the squad room and paused at the whiteboard. It had filled out fast in the last forty-eight hours. Frank and Sarah Wilson still anchored the left side. Victor Gregory had been added on the right. In the middle, someone had scrawled Department Nine, with the eight names listed beneath it.

He studied it, trying to form connections. It looked like progress but didn't feel like it. There were still too many pieces that didn't fit.

Thorpe came in around seven, unshaven and still in yesterday's clothes.

"Rough night?" Savage remarked dryly.

"Sorry, Sheriff. I stayed at Grace's. She's... she's still shaken up about the Wilsons. They held a vigil at the high school last night."

Savage grimaced. He should've read it the second Thorpe walked in. Lack of sleep, he told himself, but it wasn't a great excuse.

"Sorry," he muttered, and took his coffee into his office.

A short while later, he heard Sinclair come in, followed by Barb. Their voices carried from the front—something about a wedding, a planner—then a quick burst of laughter before they split off to their desks. It struck him how the mood at the station lifted as they came in, the place easing out of its early-morning quiet.

Sinclair popped her head around his open door. "Morning, Sheriff. You're in early."

He nodded. "Plenty to get through. Murderer to catch."

She smiled. "Amen to that."

Lucas came in last, though not by much. Savage didn't need to look up to know it was him. The uneven rhythm of his boots on the wooden floor on account of his limp gave him away. It was barely noticeable most of the time.

Clara had mentioned there was still shrapnel in Lucas's leg, too deep to safely remove. Savage knew it flared up now and then, especially in the cold, but Lucas never complained. Never even acknowledged it.

Savage let them get settled, focusing instead on Robert Carver, the State Department agent who'd leaned on Zales to shut down the CIA investigation into Department Nine. What he found didn't improve his mood.

Carver had died four years previously from heart failure, or so his death certificate said. According to the obituary in the *Chicago Tribune*, he'd been retired for about eight years by then and living in Tucson.

Given the man's age, that wasn't unusual, but then heart failure was easy enough to mimic if someone knew what they were doing and had the right resources.

Savage leaned back in his chair, scowling at the screen. He''d been hoping Carver might fill in some of the gaps that Zales'' case folder hadn''t, but it looked like that was a dead end. Literally.

Another name that couldn't answer questions. Or worse, one that had been made sure it couldn't. He made a mental note to look into it some more.

His cell phone buzzed.

Picking it up, he read the message and felt his pulse quicken. Tomahawk had come through. He'd sent him the name of the businessman from the elevator footage.

Larry Quince.

The hotel booking had been made under the name of a company called Equinox Holdings. Why did that name ring a bell?

He did a quick internet search and snorted. Equinox Holdings was a data center provider based out of D.C. They specialized in planning and constructing large-scale facilities, site assessment, infrastructure development, and project management.

He'd bet his trigger finger that they were here to meet with Caldwell.

"Got a lead on one of the men on the surveillance footage," he told the others, walking into the squad room. "Businessman named Quince. He works for Equinox Holdings."

He heard Thorpe's fingers fly over his keyboard.

"Thought I recognized the name. They're the construction company that won the bid to build the data center, if the proposal gets approved."

Savage nodded. "That's right. Thought I'd go and have a word with Quince."

"Want company?" Lucas asked.

Savage gave a nod.

"Where are we on Gregory?" he asked the team. "Anything new?"

Thorpe never took his eyes off his screen. "Not much, and what there is, doesn't give us a lot to work with. Arthur Renner is a solid alias, been in use for at least twelve years, driver's license issued in Nevada, currently registered to an apartment in Aurora. No wife, no kids, no family connections that I can find."

"So he changed his name?" Sinclair asked.

Thorpe frowned. "Not officially. Must have used a fake ID to get a driver's license."

"What about the vehicle he had at the casino?" Savage asked.

"That was a rental, hired in his assumed name."

Savage noticed Lucas frowning.

"What's up?"

"Nothing. It's just Gregory had no family attachments, no footprint worth speaking of. He was living under an assumed alias. Seems like he's been flying under the radar for a long time."

"You think he might still have been active?" Savage wondered. It was a fairly typical profile for an assassin.

Lucas shrugged. "Not a lot of work out there for former mercenaries. He might be freelancing. Earning extra on the side."

"Except someone took him out," Sinclair reminded them. "In exactly the same way as the Wilsons. Are we saying there were *two* hitmen for hire in our town?"

There was a brief pause.

"Could be retaliation?" Lucas suggested. "For the Wilsons."

Savage frowned. "That would imply somebody knew he was the shooter."

Lucas gave a tight nod. "It would."

"Could be the person who hired him," Sinclair suggested.

Savage rubbed his jaw. He'd neglected to shave that morning, and it felt like it. "It's a possibility," he agreed.

"But why use the same method?" Lucas leaned forward in his chair. "That's what I don't get. It was exactly the same. That's not a coincidence. That's someone leaving a message."

Thorpe stretched out his long legs. "Maybe whoever killed Gregory was trained in the same way he was."

"Two of them," Lucas said with a slow nod. "Two operators from the same unit, both here at the same time."

"If they're from the same unit, why is one of them killing the other?" Sinclair asked.

"Could be one was sent to do the job," Savage said, thinking aloud, "and the other was sent to make sure there was no loose end afterward. Clean the cleaner. Same as what they did in Iraq."

"That's a deeply disturbing thought," Thorpe said.

"Yeah," Savage agreed. "It is."

He pulled out his keys and nodded at McBride. "Let's go. You two, keep at it. See what you can dig up on our second hitman. I'm going to find Larry Quince."

FOURTEEN

WHILE SAVAGE WENT in search of Larry Quince, Lucas drifted through the casino.

Alongside Quince's name, Tomahawk had sent over a list of the other fifth-floor guests, complete with driver's license photos. Including Victoria Davis. Mid-twenties, Austin-based, and listed as a pharmaceutical rep. She'd been the guest in room 508. And unlike the others, she was still checked in.

The gaming floor was busy even at this hour. The morning crowd was thinner than the evening rush but just as committed. Slot machines pinged and chattered in their relentless way, and the air smelled of coffee, stale perfume, and recycled air conditioning.

A cocktail waitress moved between the tables with a practiced smile and a tray of drinks that nobody needed at ten in the morning but that several people accepted anyway. The roulette wheel spun at one table, the ball skittering around its track like it had been dropped on a hard floor.

He found Victoria Davis at a row of slot machines near the far wall, holding a paper cup of quarters. She fed them in with the absent rhythm of someone who was killing time rather than expecting to win.

Shooting her a grin, he sat down beside her. "You have a minute?"

It was impossible to disguise who he was, seeing as he was in uniform. He saw her gaze falter as she took in his deputy badge, but then she forced a smile on her face.

"How can I help you, Deputy?" She had a soft southern accent.

"I'm sorry to bother you, Miss Davis."

Her eyebrow arched. "You know my name?"

"We do. I need to ask you some questions about your stay, if that's okay?"

She tilted her head and smiled. "It wasn't that bad, but sure. Ask away." Her heavily made-up eyes glimmered in the fluorescent lighting.

He chortled. "Thanks. I wanted to ask if you heard anything unusual on your floor two nights ago. There was an incident, and we're speaking to all the guests on that level."

She shook her head. "No, I don't think so. What time are we talking about?"

"Sometime after ten in the evening, before three in the morning." It was a guestimate. They didn't have the official time of death yet.

"I was probably asleep by then," she said, with a rueful grin. "I go to bed pretty early on account of my job."

"Which is?" he asked.

"I'm a pharmaceutical rep. Eye products."

"Ophthalmologic?" he asked.

"Huh?"

Pharma rep, my ass, Lucas thought.

"What's your company called?"

He saw her eyes shift as she tried to think of something.

He saved her the trouble. "Listen, Victoria. I know you're not a pharmaceutical rep. Honestly, I don't care what you're doing in this hotel. It's not my concern. I do care, however, about this guy." He held up his phone showing a picture of Larry Quince, taken from the construction company's website. "He was on your floor that night, which is mighty strange considering he checked into a room on the second floor."

She didn't say anything, just stared at the phone with a guarded look in her eyes.

A slot machine nearby erupted into a jangle of electronic celebration as someone two stools down hit a minor jackpot. Neither of them looked at it.

"It's important you tell me if you saw him the other night," Lucas continued, after a beat. "Because a man was murdered a few doors down from you, and at the moment, this guy is the prime suspect."

She gasped. "Murdered."

A few people glanced in their direction.

"You might want to keep your voice down," Lucas advised quietly. "Now, was he with you?"

She glanced at the phone, then at the slot machine, then back at the phone. He could see the calculation going on, the weighing of one kind of trouble against another.

"Was he a client?" he pressed.

The roulette ball clattered and settled somewhere behind them. A man at the blackjack table let out a low groan.

She gave a reluctant nod.

Lucas exhaled. "Good. You're doing great, Victoria."

She gave a half-smile.

"Now, can you tell me what time he was with you?"

She frowned, trying to remember. "I—Um..."

"Was it around midnight?" That was the timestamp on the footage, according to the sheriff. That's when Quince had been on the elevator landing, umming and ahhing about going to Victoria's room.

"Yeah, I think it was," she said, clicking her fingers.

"And when did he leave?"

"About two," she said. "Maybe just after."

That tracked.

"Okay," Lucas said, pocketing his phone. "That's all I needed. You've been very helpful, Victoria. Thank you."

She relaxed, the tension seeping out of her shoulders. "You know, you're not so bad for law enforcement."

"I'll take that," he said with a grin, standing up.

"Thanks for not hauling me in," she called after him.

He gave her a brief nod and walked back across the gaming floor, past the slot machines and the roulette table and the cocktail waitress with her tray.

Quince might have been acting strangely, but it had nothing to do with murdering Victor Gregory. He'd been wrestling with his conscience on that landing, but the lure of what Victoria Davis was selling had been too great to refuse.

He pulled out his phone to call Savage.

FIFTEEN

SAVAGE FOUND Quince in the hotel restaurant, a bright, carpeted room off the main lobby where the breakfast buffet was still out. He was working his way through eggs and coffee, his laptop open on the table beside him.

Mid-forties, broad-shouldered, with a head of thick, dark hair. He wore a charcoal jacket over a pressed shirt and had a quality watch on his wrist.

He looked up when Savage approached, clocked the badge, and closed the laptop with a snap.

"Mr. Quince," Savage said, pulling out the chair across from him and sitting down without being invited. "Sheriff Dalton Savage, Hawk's Landing. I was hoping to catch you before you headed out."

Quince glanced at his watch. "I've got a meeting in an hour, Sheriff. I can give you twenty minutes."

"That should do it," Savage said pleasantly.

A waitress appeared, and Savage asked for coffee. When she'd gone, he looked at Quince. "What are you doing here?"

Quince set down his fork. "You mean at the casino?"

"I mean in the county."

He cleared his throat. "I work for a company called Equinox Holdings. I'm conducting preliminary site assessments for the proposed data center. This isn't my first visit."

"You always stay at the Ridgewater Casino?" Savage asked.

"Yeah. I like it here." He frowned. "Is that a problem?"

"Depends."

"On what?"

"On what you were doing on the fifth floor two nights ago. You're booked into room 238 on the second floor, but hotel surveillance footage has you on the fifth-floor landing at twelve a.m. and then leaving in the elevator at two twenty-three in the morning. I'd like to know why."

Quince was quiet for a moment, his hands flat on the table on either side of his plate.

"I was visiting a friend," he said carefully.

"A friend on the fifth floor?"

"That's right."

Savage gave him a long, hard stare. The breakfast buffet clattered somewhere behind him as a member of staff refreshed the serving trays. A couple at the next table were talking in low voices about their plans for the day.

"The reason I'm asking, is that a man was found dead in a room on that floor. Same night. So, I need to account for everyone who was up there."

Quince stared at him. "Dead? As in murdered?"

"Shot, yes."

He leaned back in his chair and ran a hand through his hair. "Whoa! I didn't have anything to do with that. I swear, I was with... my friend all night."

"Not all night," Savage said. "You left just after two in the morning."

"Yes. Yes."

"What time did you arrive?"

"It was around midnight."

"Can your friend confirm that?"

"Yeah." A beat. "But I'd rather you didn't ask her."

Her.

Savage frowned and moved on. "You seemed uncertain on the footage. You stood on the landing for a while before you proceeded down the corridor."

Quince picked up his coffee cup, found it empty, and set it back down.

"I was trying to decide whether it was a good idea," he said, eventually. "You know?"

"And you decided it was."

Quince shrugged. "Yeah."

Savage's coffee arrived. He thanked the waitress and waited until she'd gone.

"Why are you here?" he asked, reaching for it.

"That data center," Quince said, without preamble. "My company has been hired to conduct a preliminary survey of the land."

"Tell me about that." Savage took a sip and leaned back in his chair. He hoped the conversational tone would relax Quince enough to let down his guard some more.

Quince straightened up. "The site is about four hundred acres of former ranch land, well-situated for what we need. Good road access, proximity to the power grid, low population density. From a construction standpoint it's about as straightforward as a project this size gets."

Savage could tell that this was ground he was more comfortable on.

"And the facility itself?"

"Large scale. Server buildings, cooling infrastructure, backup power systems. The kind of operation the hyper scalers are investing in heavily and will continue to invest in for the foreseeable future."

"Sounds awful."

Quince spread his hands. "Sheriff, this is the infrastructure the modern world depends on. Streaming, navigation, banking—it all runs on data, and that data has to be processed somewhere. AI is only accelerating the demand. Faster systems, bigger workloads, more power. It doesn't come out of thin air.

"And you decided this seemed like a good place?" Savage asked, narrowing his gaze.

"I didn't decide, no. The Powers That Be decided. My company just got called in to do the assessment."

Savage found he was scowling. He didn't like that answer any better.

"Think of the jobs, Sheriff," Quince went on, clocking his reaction. "A center like this will need technical staff, security, facilities management. For a town the size of Hawk's Landing, that's a meaningful number of positions."

Savage thought about the burned hillsides above town, the farmers who hadn't recovered from the summer, the businesses on Main Street that hadn't put their Halloween decorations up because they couldn't afford them.

He thought about Clara McBride wielding her shotgun, the protests by some of the townsfolk, and about what four hundred acres of server buildings would look like against the mountains.

"I was surveying the site a couple of days ago, actually," Quince said, warming to the topic. Like he wanted to keep the Sheriff talking about this subject rather than the last one. "With Mr. Caldwell and the development team. We conducted a preliminary ground survey, or at least we were trying to when we got interrupted by a woman on horseback with a shotgun who made it very clear we weren't welcome."

"I am aware. Caldwell lodged a complaint."

"Good. Damn crazy woman." He dragged a hand through his hair. "I've done site assessments in some challenging environments, Sheriff, but that was the first time I've been scared off by a gun-toting local."

It probably wouldn't be the last, he thought sagely.

Savage's phone buzzed in his jacket. He checked the screen, then held up a hand. "Excuse me, I've got to take this."

Quince nodded as Savage stepped away from the table and walked toward the window.

"Lucas?" he said quietly. "Did you find her?"

"Yep. She confirmed Quince was with her from around midnight until just after two. He's got a solid alibi for the night of the murder."

"Understood. Thanks."

Pocketing his phone, Savage returned to the table and sat down. "Seems your friend on the fifth floor vouched for you."

Quince blinked. "She did?"

"Yeah. Victoria Davis, right?"

Quince glanced down at the table. "She said her name was Vicky. That's all I know."

"Well, you should thank her. She just cleared you as a suspect."

He heaved a sigh of relief. "Thank God."

"I noticed you've got your wedding ring back on, Mr. Quince."

A long silence.

"I'm not going to make this any more difficult than it needs to be," Savage stood up. "You have an alibi for the night of the shooting, so you're free to go. However, if you ever feel the need to engage the services of Miss Davis again, I'll make sure your wife hears about it. Are we clear?"

Quince nodded hastily. "Yes, sir. I mean, Sheriff."

Savage gave a curt nod. "Send my regards to Mr. Caldwell."

He walked out through the lobby and into the cool morning. Lucas leaned against the Suburban with his arms folded.

"Clean?" Lucas asked.

"Clean," Savage said, unlocking the truck. "Let's get back to the department."

SIXTEEN

TOMAHAWK ARRIVED at the sheriff's department just after noon.

Savage got to his feet as Barbara showed him through without being asked.

"Tomahawk, what brings you by?" He gestured to the vacant chair opposite.

Tomahawk sat down. "Thought you might like an update."

"Appreciate that." Savage eased himself back down.

"Feds shut down the entire floor for twenty-four hours after you discovered the body," he said with a derisive snort. "Casino practically cleared out. Sam Walking Deer was furious."

"They must have lost a lot of business," Savage commented.

Tomahawk nodded. "At least the staff still got paid, but the casino took a hit."

Given the amount of revenue the casino generated, Savage was sure they could handle it.

"Anyone we know?" he asked.

Tomahawk shrugged. "Two agents out of the Denver field office. Hendricks and Park."

Savage shook his head. He didn't recognize those names.

"They took one look at the body and made it clear it was a federal matter." He paused. "Which it is, technically. Can't argue with them there. Non-native victim on tribal land, that's FBI jurisdiction under the Major Crimes Act."

Savage knew how it worked. It wasn't the first time they'd been in this position.

"They take the body?" he asked.

"Yeah. Transported to the federal medical examiner in Denver. They pulled all the surveillance footage, the hotel records, and interviewed Jonas and the staff." He settled back in his chair. "They're thorough, I'll give them that."

"They'll know he was booked in under Arthur Renner," Savage muttered.

Tomahawk gave him a sharp look. "I take it that wasn't the victim's real name?"

"You got that right," he admitted, running a hand through his hair.

"Well, they'll run that alias through every federal database they have access to." He said it without malice, just as a statement of fact.

Savage gave an unimpressed grunt. "Hopefully, they won't make the connection."

That would leave him free to continue with his investigation. If the Feds did piece it all together, link it with the double homicide in Hawk's Landing, then they might muscle in on the whole thing.

"I believe you spoke to Larry Quince?" Tomahawk said.

Savage raised an eyebrow across the desk. "He tell you that?"

"Jonas Half Moon saw you having coffee together this morning."

"We had a chat."

"Get anywhere?" Tomahawk asked. At Savage's suspicious look, he shrugged. "Call it professional curiosity. I'm interested to know who shot Renner. It was on my land, after all."

"Fair enough." He'd want to know too, if it were him. "Turns out Mr. Quince was engaging the services of a lady on the fifth floor the night of the murder. We spoke to her, and she vouched for him."

Tomahawk chuckled. "Well, well... I'm sure Sam Walking Deer will be interested to know that."

"Figured it was none of my business," Savage said with a shrug.

"But it is his," Tomahawk murmured. "Soliciting is illegal on the res too."

Savage switched gears. "Did the FBI ask about my investigation?"

"Nope, and I didn't mention it." Tomahawk shrugged. "Not my jurisdiction."

Savage grinned. "Thanks for that."

Tomahawk broke into a rare smile. "Save your thanks for this."

Savage raised his eyebrows while Tomahawk reached into his jacket and produced a folded piece of paper. He set it on the desk.

"A list of all the guests staying on the floor the night of the shooting."

Savage glanced up. "How'd you get this?"

"Jonas gave it to Hendricks, but I got a copy first. By the way, they were all seen on camera at some point during that evening."

"That makes sense since most got back to their rooms after two on the morning." He gave a wry smile. "But thanks for checking it out. We'll look into them anyway."

"There was one other thing I didn't mention to the FBI."

"Oh, yeah?"

"When we went through the full guest list against the elevator footage, there was one individual Jonas couldn't account for. Native American. Ponytail. You remember him from the footage?"

Savage nodded. "He wasn't staying at the hotel?"

"No. But one of the dealers knew him. Goes by the name Joe Grinning Bear."

"He live on the res?" Savage asked.

"Yep."

"You got an address?"

"I do. But just so we're clear, you've got no jurisdiction on reservation land. You can't arrest him for anything that happened out there."

Savage spread his hands over the desk. “I just want to ask him some questions.”

“Then I come with you,” Tomahawk said, in a tone that made clear it wasn’t a suggestion. “My people don’t respond well to county law enforcement showing up unannounced. Especially in connection with a murder.”

“Fair enough,” Savage said.

“I’ll be in touch about when.” Tomahawk got to his feet. “Be seeing you, Sheriff.”

After he’d gone, Savage set the piece of paper on Thorpe’s desk. “I’ve got a list of all the guests on the fifth floor the night of the murder.”

“That’s great,” Sinclair said, glancing up. “Tomahawk come through for us?”

Savage nodded. “Joe Grinning Bear. Give me everything you can find on him.”

“Who is he?” Thorpe asked.

“He’s an unknown,” he told him. “Wasn’t staying at the hotel and so had no reason to be on that floor.”

“How’d you know who he was?” Thorpe, ever astute, asked.

“Dealer knew him.”

Thorpe nodded and got to work.

“Is this Joe Grinning Bear the only one unaccounted for?” Lucas asked.

“Yeah, although he didn’t look to be carrying on the surveillance footage.”

“Could have stashed the weapon in one of the rooms,” Lucas said.

“Or in a hall closet or something,” Sinclair added.

Savage turned to go back to his office. “True. Either way, we need to find out what he was doing there.”

“Sheriff?” Thorpe called, halting him.

“Yeah? What you got?”

"Joseph Grinning Bear has a criminal record. Possession with intent to distribute, back in 2014. He served eighteen months."

"Shit, really?" Sinclair murmured.

"That's not all." Thorpe read down the list. "Aggravated assault, 2018. The charges were eventually reduced, and he took a fine. By the looks of things, he's kept his nose clean since then."

"He employed?" Savage asked.

"Nothing formal. There's no vehicle registered in his name."

"How'd he get to the casino if he doesn't have a car?" Lucas pointed out.

"Probably not registered to him," Savage muttered.

"How's he supporting himself if he's not working?" Sinclair asked.

"Illegally would be my guess." Savage took out his phone. "Suppose I'll be seeing Tomahawk again sooner than either of us expected."

SEVENTEEN

THEY TOOK Savage's Suburban out to the reservation, following Tomahawk's cruiser south on a two-lane blacktop that cut through open country. The town fell away behind them, replaced by long stretches of sagebrush, barbed-wire fences, and the occasional weathered trailer set back from the road. The mesa rose dark to the south, its flanks catching the last of the light while the sky above them stretched wide and pale.

Sinclair sat in the passenger seat with her window cracked open despite the cold, her elbow resting against the door as she watched the scenery whiz by.

"Do you really think Grinning Bear could have done it?" she asked.

Savage kept his eyes on the road ahead, watching the flicker of Tomahawk's taillights as the cruiser crested a slight rise.

"I don't know. Seems like a hell of a coincidence that he was loitering fifty yards from a dead assassin, though."

"Maybe he was avenging the Wilsons?" She turned away from the window to look at him.

"We don't know Gregory killed the Wilsons," Savage cautioned, squinting into the distance. "He may have been at the casino for an entirely different reason, and somebody else killed all three of them."

Sinclair let out a frustrated breath.

Ahead of them, Tomahawk's brake lights flared before his vehicle turned off the blacktop onto a narrower road that branched away from the highway.

The asphalt gave way to a rougher, patched surface before finally thinning into a worn strip of compacted dirt and gravel that wound toward a small cluster of buildings set back from the road.

The Suburban rocked slightly as Savage followed, easing off the gas. Dust lifted behind Tomahawk's cruiser in a pale cloud that drifted across the scrub.

The property came into view as they approached. A single-story house sat low against the land, its paint faded and peeling in places. A rusted pickup truck was parked out front with its hood up, as if it had been left mid-repair. Two outbuildings stood behind the house, both in poor shape, their tin roofs dulled and dented, doors hanging unevenly on their hinges.

A dog chained near the front yard caught sight of them before they had come to a stop and began barking, a sharp, relentless sound that carried across the open ground.

Savage killed the engine and stepped out, the cool fall air hitting him immediately. The smell out here was different from town, dry and dusty with a faint trace of woodsmoke drifting from somewhere nearby.

Tomahawk raised a hand without turning around, signaling them to hold back, and walked toward the front door alone.

SAVAGE WATCHED HIM GO, then turned to Sinclair and gave a small gesture toward the side of the house. She nodded without a word and moved off, circling wide to cover the rear. The tribal police chief knocked on the door, calling out to the occupant, identifying himself.

There was no response.

The dog continued barking, straining against its chain, claws digging into the dirt as it lunged forward and snapped at the air.

Tomahawk knocked again, louder this time.

Savage shifted, bracing himself. Something was off.

Then came the sudden crash of a door slamming somewhere at the back of the house, followed almost immediately by Sinclair's voice.

"Stop! Police!"

Savage was already moving.

"He's running!" he shouted to Tomahawk as he broke into a sprint around the side of the house.

He rounded the corner and caught sight of Sinclair ahead of him, already in pursuit, her boots kicking up dust as she drove forward.

Grinning Bear was running hard, his movements quick but uncoordinated with panic. He angled toward the outbuildings as if they might offer him cover.

Beyond them, the land opened into nothing but scrub and dry grass that stretched flat and exposed to the horizon. There were no trees, no structures, nothing but wire fencing and the occasional rusted trough half buried in the earth.

It was open country. Nowhere to disappear.

Sinclair cleared the corner of the nearest outbuilding and vanished from view.

Shit.

Savage pushed harder, Tomahawk close behind him. The chained dog was in a frenzy now, barking and lunging as they passed, its chain rattling violently as it reared up onto its hind legs.

Savage rounded the outbuilding just in time to see Sinclair closing the distance on the suspect. Grinning Bear had already abandoned the structures and was heading straight for the scrub line at the edge of the property, his shoulders pumping as he ran.

He was not going to make it.

Sinclair gained on him with each stride. Ten yards from the

brush, she lunged forward and caught hold of his jacket, yanking him off balance.

For a brief moment, it looked like it was over.

Then Grinning Bear spun around, and Savage caught a glint of something in his hand. His heart skipped a beat.

"Knife!" he yelled.

But the warning came a fraction too late.

Sinclair drove into him, tackling Grinning Bear to the ground with force, the two of them hitting hard in a spray of dust and gravel. They rolled once before she forced him face down, her knee planted firmly in the middle of his back as she wrenched his arm behind him.

Grinning Bear struggled, a sharp, desperate movement, but his burst of resistance was already fading.

Savage closed the distance quickly, eyes searching for the weapon. He spotted it a few feet away, the blade catching the last light as it lay half-buried in the dirt. He kicked it farther out of reach, sending it skidding across the ground.

"You okay?" he asked.

Sinclair nodded, breathing hard, but something about the way she held her arm caught his attention.

Blood seeped through a tear in her jacket sleeve, dark against the fabric, running down toward her hand in a steady line.

"Shit!" Savage said, his voice tightening. "You're not. You're hurt."

"Well, I got him," she replied through clenched teeth.

Tomahawk arrived moments later, already pulling his handcuffs from his belt. "I'll take it from here."

Sinclair shifted her weight and released the suspect, allowing Tomahawk to take control. He wrestled Grinning Bear's other arm behind his back and snapped on the cuffs.

Savage reached out and helped Sinclair to her feet.

"Let me see that," he ordered.

She hesitated, then pulled her arm away from her side. The sleeve was torn open from mid-forearm toward the wrist, the fabric soaked through with blood. Beneath it, the cut was clean but deep, a narrow opening exposing pale tissue beneath the surface.

“Damn,” he said quietly. “You’ll need stitches.”

She clenched her jaw, looking more annoyed than shaken, and nodded before pressing her arm against her ribs to stem the bleeding. Then she fixed Grinning Bear with a hard, simmering look.

“Nice move, asshole,” she snapped. “Real smart. Now you’re under arrest for assault as well as resisting arrest.”

Grinning Bear said nothing.

Tomahawk hauled him to his feet and began a quick search, his hands moving methodically over the suspect’s pockets and waistband. From one pocket, he pulled a small plastic bag filled with white powder. From another, a second bag containing what appeared to be methamphetamine crystals.

“Well, look at this,” Tomahawk said, holding the items up.

Savage snorted. “Seems like you’ll be adding possession with intent to that list of charges.”

Tomahawk gave a brief nod. Jurisdiction here was clear, and he would handle the processing on tribal land. That part was not in question.

“Once you’ve done that, I want him transferred to my custody. He assaulted one of my deputies.”

Tomahawk paused, considering it, his gaze shifting briefly to Sinclair’s arm before returning to Savage.

After a moment, he nodded. “Fair enough.”

Savage led a bleeding Sinclair to the Suburban, but she shook off his hand.

“I’m fine, honestly.”

He could tell by her clenched jaw and pale complexion that she wasn’t, but he nodded and released her good arm.

He opened the passenger door for her, then circled the vehicle and got behind the wheel. The engine turned over with a low rumble, and he cranked the heat up.

"Going to take you to La Plata County Medical Center. Get that looked at."

Sinclair leaned back in the seat, injured arm pressed against her side, jaw set as she stared out through the windshield.

Savage headed for the highway. The medical center was the nearest facility with an emergency department, and it would take a good hour to get there.

EIGHTEEN

BY THE TIME Savage got back to the sheriff's department a little after midnight, Tomahawk had been as good as his word. Joe Grinning Bear was in the holding cell, waiting for his second interrogation of the night.

Lucas was on shift, slouched in his chair, trawling through the criminal database. He'd processed, photographed, and given their suspect the opportunity to call a lawyer, which he'd apparently declined.

Probably couldn't afford one and didn't trust any that would be offered.

"How's Sinclair?" Lucas asked, looking up.

"She'll be okay." He'd left her at the medical center with a wad of gauze from the first aid kit pressed against her forearm, waiting to be seen by a doctor.

Savage nodded in the direction of the cells. "How long's he been here?"

"Not long."

Savage went into his office, put together an interview folder on the suspect, then took it with him to the cell.

"Keep an eye on us," he said to Lucas, as he walked past.

"Of course," his deputy replied. The live feed could be watched on anyone's terminal, provided they were logged into the software.

Before he went in, Savage stood in the corridor and studied Grinning Bear through the narrow window in the door. Mid-forties, lean and angular, with long dark hair and a weathered face with sharp angles and a silver scar visible on his chin. Could have been a user at some point, judging by the slim build and generally unhealthy complexion.

Savage gripped the interview folder, took a breath, and pushed open the door.

Grinning Bear watched him sit down and said nothing. This wasn't his first run-in with the law, according to his rap sheet. The guy knew the drill and wasn't saying anything he didn't have to.

Savage set the folder on the table, folded his hands on top of it, and looked at him.

"You want anything? Water, coffee?"

Nothing.

"Okay." Savage leaned back in his chair. "Let's start with what you were doing at the Ridgewater Casino on the night of November fourth?"

Grinning Bear's jaw tightened. "I thought this was about the assault on your deputy?"

"Oh, we'll get there," he said, glad he had him talking. "But you're the prime suspect in a murder investigation. Didn't my deputy tell you?"

"Murder? What the—?"

"A man was shot twice at the casino the night you were there," Savage interjected, sliding a photograph across the desk to him.

It was the crime scene photograph from room 514. Victor Gregory sat slumped in the armchair, chin to his chest, bullet holes in his jaw and temple. Not a photograph designed to make anyone comfortable, and Savage watched Grinning Bear's face carefully as he took it in.

"Hey, man. I didn't have nothing to do with any shooting."

Savage tapped the table. "This occurred on the same floor you were on. Around the same time." Although, to be fair, that still needed confirming.

Grinning Bear stared at him, a horrified expression on his face.

"We know you didn't have a room on that floor, so my question stands. What were you doing there?"

"I—I didn't shoot that guy," he stammered.

"That's not what I asked," Savage said calmly.

The man gritted his teeth. "What I was doing there is none of your business."

Savage shook his head as if he couldn't believe the stupidity of the man. From the folder, he took out a still of the surveillance footage from that night. It featured Grinning Bear standing outside the elevator, hands in his pockets.

"This you?"

The suspect glanced down at it but didn't reply.

"Doesn't matter. We can see it's you," Savage said. "You're even wearing the same shirt."

Grinning Bear looked down as if realizing it for the first time.

"Now, unless you want to go down for murder as well as assault, you'd better start talking."

"Shit," the man muttered, shifting in his chair.

"About sums it up," Savage agreed.

A long pause. Grinning Bear looked at the table. Savage could see him working through it, weighing one kind of trouble against another.

"I was there on business," he said eventually.

"You mean you were selling drugs?" Savage sat back, his arms crossed. It was as he'd expected, but he needed proof.

A slight nod, almost imperceptible.

"To whom?" Savage asked. When the suspect didn't reply, he said, "Who was your client?"

"A woman," Grinning Bear said finally, his voice dropping.

"Works out of the casino. She sometimes calls me when she's in town."

"What does she buy from you?" he asked.

"Meth," he said with a shrug. "She likes to get high before... You know?"

"No, you're going to have to explain it to me," said Savage, even though he could guess. He needed this on record.

"Before she does whatever it is hookers do," he finished.

"You got a name?" Savage asked.

Grinning Bear shrugged. "I only know her as Vicky."

Victoria Davis. That made sense.

"So, you dropped off the product, and what then?" he asked, placing his hands on the table.

"I left. Went back downstairs."

"You didn't take the elevator," Savage said. He knew from watching the stairwell footage that the drug dealer had slunk down that way, back to the casino floor.

"Don't want to be seen by too many people," he admitted, pushing out his lower lip.

The elevator went down to the mezzanine where reception was based. From there, Grinning Bear would have had to ride the escalator down to the casino floor. While the stairwell went all the way down.

He didn't tell him this, though.

"You can prove this?" he asked.

"Sheriff, I went to her door, handed her the drugs, took the cash, and left. I didn't get it in writing or anything."

"How'd she order them?" Savage asked.

"She texted me." His eyes widened. "I still got the message on my phone."

"I'll need to see it."

"Tomahawk took my phone from me when he arrested me," the dealer grumbled.

"Okay, no problem."

Tomahawk could verify the message. That's all they needed. Then they could ask Victoria Davis to give her side of the story.

If it panned out, Grinning Bear was also in the clear.

NINETEEN

THE SKY BEGAN to lighten behind the mountains, the peaks still half-hidden by mist, when Savage turned into his drive.

As Apple Tree Farm came into view, he thought about when he'd first moved here with Becca. It had been a lovely Fall day, not unlike this one would be, when they'd come to see it. He'd loved it as soon as he'd seen it. The space, the view, the peace and quiet.

They'd bought it after their house had burned to the ground in a deliberate arson attack orchestrated by his corrupt former partner. Displaced, and looking for a property that would serve as a home in which to raise their son, he'd discovered it almost by accident.

The farm had been abandoned after the previous owners fell on hard times. The bank had foreclosed on the property. He'd purchased it for a bargain price, and they moved in just before a particularly harsh winter hit the region.

He climbed out of the Suburban and gazed out at the distant purple-hued, snow-covered peaks. As far as scenery went, he'd yet to see anything more beautiful. But Becca had never been happy here.

It was too far out for her. Connor had been only a few months old when they'd moved in, and she'd felt alone and isolated. It had gotten worse after the snowstorms had made it too dangerous to drive. He knew that had contributed to her decision to leave.

When he'd signed on as sheriff for another term, that had been the final straw.

Legs heavy with weariness, he climbed the porch steps to the front door and let himself into the house. It was small, a kitchen, living room, and two bedrooms, one of them tiny, but the renovations he'd planned had been put on hold due to the harsh winter, and then when Becca had left, there hadn't seemed to be much point.

Now he simply existed in it, spending most of his time on the wide porch that stretched the entire length of the front of the house. The view was better there.

He glanced at the time. It was nearly six-thirty. Becca would be up feeding Connor, so he might be able to catch them. He knew their routine by now, sometimes mapping it out in his head when he was working.

Settling at the kitchen table, he video called Becca. She answered right away, which surprised him.

"Hey, how's it going?" he asked, drinking in the sight of her face.

She gave him a guarded smile. "Fine."

Guarded was all he got these days.

"How are you?" she asked.

"I'm good. How have you two been getting on?" He thought she looked well-rested. Connor must be sleeping through the night finally.

"Great, actually. Connor's doing well. You want to see him?"

"Yeah." He'd have liked to speak to her for longer too, but she didn't seem to want to do that.

A moment later, his son's cherubic little face filled the screen, and his heart melted. He was so goddamn beautiful. Damn, he missed him. Missed them both.

"Look. Who's that? That's Daddy," came Becca's voice over the phone.

"Hey, Connor," he said. "I'm going to come and visit you as soon as I can."

His son said something unintelligible, and Becca's face lit up.

"He's started to say a few words. Mostly nonsense, but I thought I heard him say Mama the other day."

"That's great."

When would he say Dada? Considering Savage wasn't there, that would probably come a lot later.

"You're looking good," he said to Becca, once Connor had lost interest and she'd put him down on the floor at her feet. He was crawling now, starting to pull himself up on things.

"Thanks. I got some help with Connor."

"You did?" This was news. He wasn't sure how he felt about someone else looking after their child, but then he reminded himself not to be selfish. Becca had been doing all this by herself, raising him alone for the most part. She deserved a break.

"Who?" he asked.

"A babysitter. Her name's Evelyn, and she's really good with him."

"Evelyn have a last name?"

"You're going to look her up, aren't you?"

"I think it's only fair. I'm not there to—"

"But I am, Dalton. I'm not going to hire a psycho to look after our son. You're going to have to trust me on this one."

He hissed out a breath. "Okay, fine."

"Okay?" Her eyebrow rose.

"Yes. I trust you to find the best person to look after our son."

She exhaled softly. "Thank you. Now, was that so hard?"

She always had a way of handling him, making him see sense. He used to run things by her. Cases. Suspects. Scenarios. She helped him clear his mind, put things into perspective. All that was gone now.

"I miss you," he said.

There was a short pause.

"I've got to go, Dalton."

He nodded. "Where are you going?"

"Out. We're going out for the day."

They ended the call after that, but he sat for a long time at the kitchen table, staring at the wall.

She'd said "we."

He sure as hell hoped she meant her and Connor, and not somebody else.

IT WAS mid-morning when Savage got in to work. Thorpe had both monitors running and was flicking between them. Sinclair was on the phone, her bandaged arm resting on the desk in front of her. Lucas was at his station, frowning at whatever was on his screen.

Nobody looked up when he came in, which suited him fine.

He grabbed a coffee and went into his office, closing the door behind him. Joe Grinning Bear was gone, picked up by Tomahawk and transported back to the tribal station. Lucas had followed up with Victoria Davis, who'd grudgingly admitted to sending the text message and buying half a gram off him that night.

Savage had let him go.

Grinning Bear had been arrested on the reservation, which made it Tomahawk's case to process. The assault on Sinclair would be added to the list of charges on their side. Savage could have pushed to bring him back under county custody, but it would have meant paperwork, coordination, and time he didn't have. More importantly, it would have pulled his people off what mattered. This case.

The same went for Victoria Davis. What she was doing skirted the law, and Lucas had made that clear. She'd been warned, and she'd promised to keep her business away from the casino. For now, that was enough.

They had a killer to catch. A low-level dealer with a knife was not where his attention needed to be.

Savage pulled the Zales folder toward him and had just opened it when Barbara knocked on his door. He called her in.

"Dalton, Quentin Wilson called while you were out. Said he'd been thinking about what you asked him, and he's got nothing more to add, but wanted you to know he's arranged for his parents to be buried in Hawk's Landing, at the cemetery on Birch Hill. Said it felt right. Funeral's next week."

He nodded. "Thanks, Barb."

She hovered. He looked up.

"Also," she said, in a slightly apprehensive tone, "the Wilsons' neighbors on Maple Ridge Lane have been asking when they can expect to have the street back to normal. The crime scene tape has been up for nearly a week."

"Tell them soon," he said, although he wasn't sure that was true.

She went back to her desk.

Savage studied the list of eight names. Victor Gregory was crossed out now, in his mind if not on the paper. That left seven. One of them had been in that hotel on the same night as Gregory, had let himself into Gregory's hotel room, and had put two bullets in him with the same precision that Gregory had used on the Wilsons.

Same training. Same unit. Different instructions.

Or the same instructions, and Gregory was the next job.

He was just pondering this when there was a knock on his door, and Thorpe stuck his head inside. "Sheriff, got a minute?"

"Sure, Thorpe. What's up?"

"I just spoke to Grace. She said Sarah and Frank's son never came to visit them. Not once in the last couple of years. Sarah was really cut up about it."

Savage looked up. "Quentin said he hadn't been out to visit in four months."

"Four months is not never," he said.

"Did Sarah give a reason?"

"Only to say that he'd fallen out with his father, and that she missed him terribly."

"Strange. I wonder what they fell out about?"

"I don't know, but I'm going to do a deep dive into Quentin Wilson."

If they were estranged, that was motive, Savage thought grimly.

Thorpe adjusted his glasses, then said, "I also ran his flight details through the system and guess what? He landed in Durango over a week ago."

Savage jerked his head up. "A week? So, he was here *before* his parents were killed?"

"Seems like it."

"Then why the hell didn't he say so?" Savage rubbed his jaw. Suddenly the Wilson's son wasn't looking quite so innocent anymore.

"And we know he served," Thorpe pointed out.

Means as well. The trifecta.

"Bring him in," Savage said.

TWENTY

"WHY AM I HERE?" Quentin Wilson demanded, staring at Savage across the interrogation room table. Savage had decided to forgo the pleasantries this time and opt for intimidation.

"Think about it," Savage said quietly. He saw a flicker of discomfort cross his prime suspect's face.

Good. Let him squirm.

The guy had lied about everything. There was no trust anymore. No benefit of the doubt.

"I don't know what you mean, Sheriff."

"I think you do," Savage pushed. "We know all about you, Quentin. We know when you arrived in the county. We know about your relationship with your parents, or lack thereof. We even know why. And I have to be honest with you, considering how they died, you are now at the top of our suspect list."

Quentin looked shocked, then defiant.

"I didn't have anything to do with their deaths."

"If that is true—and I have no reason to believe you anymore—then you'd better start talking, because from where I'm sitting, it sure looks like you did."

There was a long pause. Savage could see Quentin churning over his thoughts, trying to decide what to say.

"The truth is always easiest," Savage encouraged, leaning back in his chair and crossing his arms.

Quentin let out a sigh. "Okay, fine. Yeah, I got here a week ago, but not for the reason you think. I didn't want to kill them."

"Why then?"

"I wanted to talk with them about... about my biological parents. I wanted an explanation. I wanted to know why they didn't tell me who I really was."

"They adopted you." It wasn't a question. Thorpe had already uncovered this during his deep dive, along with several other interesting facts about Quentin Wilson.

The man in question nodded, jaw tense.

"They lied to me. All my life I thought I was their son. That I shared their DNA, their history. But none of that was true."

"Was that why you hadn't been to see them in"—he glanced down at the note he'd made in the file—"over three years?"

Quentin's mouth pressed into a flat line.

"You said you hadn't been here for a few months," Savage reminded him.

Quentin shifted in his chair. "That's because I knew how it would look. The estranged son returns the day before they end up dead. Obviously, I'd be the prime suspect."

Savage gave a nod of acknowledgement. "Yeah, you are. You still haven't convinced me otherwise."

He sighed. "I loved my parents, okay? It hurt that they'd lied to me, but I was dealing with it."

"That why you're seeing a therapist?" Savage asked. Another one of Thorpe's insights.

His eyes widened. "You know about that?"

"We're good at our job," was all he said.

"Yeah. Well, she told me I had to come back and confront them about it. I stormed out three years ago after I discovered the truth. I was so angry that I let my emotions get the better of me."

"How'd you find out?" Savage asked, mostly because he was curious. Why would the Wilsons feel it was important to keep something like that from their adopted son?

"A letter arrived. It was from a woman claiming to be my aunt. She said her sister, my biological mother, had passed away, and she thought I should know." He scowled across the table. "At first, I was confused. I thought it was some mistake. But when I showed them, they told me it was true. That they'd adopted me."

Savage watched him, saying nothing. Letting him talk.

"My mother was a crack whore, did you know that?" His voice was strained with emotion. "She got pregnant at eighteen and gave me up. Probably by some pimp or someone she was screwing for drugs."

Savage didn't know. That hadn't been in the adoption report.

"Makes sense why they didn't want to tell you," Savage said. "Did you ever think that maybe they had your best interests at heart?"

"I do now," he said. "I only found out about her recently, when I spoke to my aunt. Then I kind of wished I didn't know."

Savage drummed his fingers on the table. "Why didn't you speak to them when you got back?" he asked, eventually.

"I wanted to. I was just picking my moment. I hadn't seen them for so long, I needed to ease into it."

"They were your parents, I'm sure they would have understood."

"I fucked up, okay? I know that. And now it's too late. Don't you think I regret that?" He dropped his head into his hands and gave a strangled sob. "It's too damn late."

Savage watched him and let out a slow breath. Was he telling the truth? It seemed convincing enough. It explained the early flight, the absence, the personal turmoil.

But did it have anything to do with why they'd been shot?

"Do you still have this letter?" he asked, after a beat.

Quentin looked up, his gaze haunted. "Yeah, of course."

"I need to see it. I also want the name and contact details for your aunt."

"My aunt? But why?"

"To make sure she didn't have anything to do with your parents' death. She knew where they lived, obviously, judging by the letter."

"She didn't even know their names," he insisted. "The letter was addressed to me."

"Doesn't matter. You don't need to know someone's name to pull a trigger."

Four times.

Quentin gnawed on his lower lip, agitated. "Why would my aunt want to kill the couple that adopted me?"

"I'm not saying she did. I'm saying we've got to rule her out."

He sighed. "Okay. I've got her details in my phone. I can give them to you right now."

"That would be good."

Savage passed over a piece of paper and a pen, then got to his feet.

Quentin scribbled down a name and a number.

Maeve Carter.

Savage picked up the sheet and tucked it in the folder. Then he headed for the door, taking it and the pen with him.

"Hey, when can I get out of here?" Quentin called after him.

"When I've verified what you say is true."

Savage closed the door, making sure to lock it behind him.

"THE AUNT CHECKS OUT," Thorpe said, putting down his phone. "She did write the letter."

"The biological mother?" Savage asked.

"Died a year ago. Liver failure from drug and alcohol abuse."

Savage cringed.

"Why'd the aunt want to tell him that?"

Thorpe shrugged. “Money, most likely. I ran her background. She’s got priors for solicitation and shoplifting. Nothing recent, but enough to paint a picture. I think she knew her sister had a kid out there somewhere and figured it might be worth something.”

Savage leaned back in his chair. “Did he give her anything?”

Thorpe gave a small shake of his head. “Not a cent. And she’s not taking it well.” He glanced down at his notes. “Called him a ‘fancy-shmancy tight-ass.’ Her words.”

“Sounds like the Wilsons were protecting their son from his biological family,” Sinclair mused. “And he never understood why.”

It was sad. The Wilsons had showered their adopted son with love, raised him well, given him a comfortable home, and an education. Everything a kid could want. And somehow, it still hadn’t been enough.

Savage understood the need to know your roots, but all things considered, the guy didn’t know how lucky he was. He thought about his own son being raised by a single mom and felt his chest tighten.

Was that what he’d done? Thrown Becca’s lies back in her face?

Sure, she’d been untruthful with him, about something pretty big, too, but she had her reasons. It still hurt that she hadn’t trusted him enough to tell him her real name. Who she really was. But maybe he just had to get over that.

Was that how Quentin felt?

Shit.

Somehow, he had to get his family back. There must be a way they could work this out. He was prepared to do anything. He’d move, if necessary. If it would make her reconsider.

He made a mental note to bring it up with Becca the very next time he saw her. As soon as this case was over and he could get to Pagosa Springs.

“Sheriff?” Lucas was saying something.

He turned to his deputy. “Huh?”

“How long do you want to keep him locked up?”

"If everything checks out, you can let him go. Tell him not to leave town, though. Not until we've got this thing tied up." Which could be a while.

"Sure thing," Lucas said.

"That leaves us with nothing," Thorpe said, looking over at Savage. "No suspects."

It was true. They'd ruled out the suspicious lurkers on the fifth floor, including Joe Grinning Bear. Now Quentin Wilson.

It was time to dig a little deeper.

"Okay, we need to look at this again." Savage ran a hand through his hair. "Let's go through that list of names Zales gave us again. Someone else from that squad is here in Hawk's Landing. We need to find him."

"I'll get right on it," Thorpe said with a nod.

Savage glanced around at Sinclair and Lucas. "I need you two to look into those guests at the hotel again. Analyze everyone on that floor. Even the ones Tomahawk confirmed were on the gaming floor. I want to see that footage. Lucas, get over there and make sure they haven't missed anything."

"On it," he said, getting up.

"Why don't I swing by the Wilsons' place and talk to the neighbors again," Sinclair volunteered. "Not that I don't trust Lucas, but someone might remember something helpful."

"Good idea," he said with a nod.

Barbara emerged from her office. "Er, Sheriff. Mrs. Herbert's been caught shoplifting again."

He sighed. At eighty-two, no one had figured out if the woman was just forgetful or using her age as an excuse to steal merchandise.

"Where this time?"

"The outdoor store on South Park Street."

"That's on the way to my place," Sinclair said. "I'll take it."

"Go home after that," Savage said, noticing how she'd cringed when she'd gotten up. The doc had put ten stitches in her arm, and it must still hurt. Besides, she had O'Riley waiting for her.

"You can stop by the Wilson place on your way in tomorrow morning."

She looked like she was about to argue, then thought better of it.

"Sure, no problem."

He didn't miss the approving nod Barbara gave him as Sinclair walked out.

TWENTY-ONE

IT HAD RAINED MOST of the night, with localized flooding causing havoc across the county. Savage had stopped on the way into work to help a farmer whose pickup had slid off the Durango road, spilling a load of pumpkins into a ditch.

By the time he arrived at the office, he was wet and covered in mud, but he was still earlier than most of the others. Only Lucas was at his desk when he walked in.

"How'd it go at the casino?" he asked, as he pulled a spare pair of jeans out of the supply closet. They all kept additional clothes at work since you never knew where this job would take you. "Was Jonas helpful?"

"Yeah, surprisingly so. He let me see the footage," Lucas said. "Quite the setup they've got there."

"Necessary in a casino. Find anything?"

Lucas straightened. "I went through all six guests on that floor and put names to faces. The two who were definitely in their rooms at the time of the murder were Victoria Davis and Thomas Harrow."

"Which one is he?"

"The old guy."

Savage nodded.

"Everybody's statements match the timestamps on the surveillance footage," Lucas went on. "Victoria Davis went up at eleven thirty, got her delivery shortly after that by Joe Running Deer, then entertained Larry Quince from midnight to about twenty past two. All three accounts check out."

"Fair enough. What about the old guy?"

Lucas consulted his notes. "Thomas Harrow. He was there the entire evening. Went up at seven thirty-five, ordered room service a little after eight. Burger and fries, according to the kitchen staff. It was delivered at eight twenty, and he came to the door himself. Said he almost didn't hear them since the TV was plugged into his hearing aid."

Savage frowned. "Could he have slipped out?"

"It's possible, I guess, but the guy's stone deaf and can't walk without his stick. Gave his address as a retirement home outside Bayfield."

Savage sighed. "Okay, doesn't sound like he's our guy either. Who else?"

Lucas glanced down again. "You've got Marcus Delaney. Plays high-stakes poker, travels the circuit. He was at the main table most of the night. We've got him on camera from early evening through to about four in the morning. Barely left his seat except to grab a drink."

"Serious player, then?"

"Yeah. He went all night."

Savage nodded.

"Then there's Daniel White Elk," Lucas continued. "He's a local, in his mid-twenties. In and out of blackjack. Nothing unusual there. He was bouncing between tables with a friend, chasing losses by the look of it. Cameras have him and his buddy on the floor until just after two."

"Friend's name?"

"Tyler Jenkins. Early twenties. Came in with White Elk, although he didn't stay over at the hotel. They stuck together most of the night, arguing a couple of times from what security said. Nothing violent, just frustration."

Savage grunted. He knew how that went. Losing didn't bring out the best in people.

"How come the kid was staying at the casino hotel?"

"Used his parents' credit card."

Savage gave a snort. "I bet that went down well."

Lucas gave a wry grin and turned a page.

"Last one's Renee Baptiste. She came down around nine, spent time at the bar, then settled at the blackjack table. She was also on camera most of the night."

Savage nodded, sensing there was more. "And?"

"Probably nothing, but she got talking to one of the other players. They left together around two-thirty. Camera caught them heading up in the elevator."

Savage frowned. "She picked him up at the table?"

"Looks that way. Guy stayed the night. Left her room just after six that morning, or that's when we caught him on the fifth-floor landing waiting for the elevator. She checked out around ten."

Savage rubbed his jaw. He recalled the impatient guy striding toward the elevator in the early hours. "Do we know who he is?"

Lucas shook his head. "No, we do not. He paid cash, won a little, nothing crazy. They had a good time, though. We've got him on camera, but no ID yet. I've stuck his picture up on the board."

Savage turned and studied it.

The guy was mid-to-late thirties, hard to tell exactly. The face was hardy, the kind you got from working outdoors or too much time on the road. Short brown hair, clean-shaven.

He glossed over the rest of him.

Nothing stood out. No visible tattoos, no jewelry, no corporate logos or sports badges. His clothes were plain. Dark jacket, jeans, boots. Average height. Average build.

Savage frowned. He was the kind of man you could pass ten times in a day and never remember.

"I don't like it. An unidentified man spends the night in a guest's room and walks out the next morning," he said. "There are no cameras in the hallway, so we don't know whether he was there all night, or if he left, took care of Gregory in room 514, then went back again."

Lucas gave a small nod. "That about sums it up."

Savage kept his eyes on the image a moment longer. "Let's find him."

SAVAGE PERCHED on Sinclair's desk while Lucas called the hotel guest, Renee Baptiste. She'd booked on a corporate card and the driver's license she'd given the hotel was registered in Albuquerque.

She picked up on the second ring.

"Ms. Baptiste, this is Deputy McBride with the Hawk's Landing Sheriff's Office. I'm calling in relation to your recent stay at Ridgewater Casino."

There was a brief pause.

"What about it?"

"We're following up on an incident that took place the evening you were there, and we're speaking to guests who were on the same floor. I just have a few questions."

"Okay." She drew out the word, like she was considering this.

He cleared his throat.

"Do you mind if I ask why you were staying at the hotel?"

"Sure. I'm a regional sales rep for a home decor company. I spend most of my time on the road, moving between cities and trade shows. I had meetings in your cute little town."

Lucas met Savage's gaze, but he just shrugged. It was cute and little. That didn't mean bad stuff didn't happen here.

"You met a man at the blackjack table," Lucas said, moving on with his questions. "We're trying to identify him."

"Oh, that would be Colton. He was a sweetheart."

"You know his last name?"

A pause. "No, actually I don't think he gave it to me. We played a few hands, had a couple of drinks. Flirted a little."

"And he spent the night with you?" Lucas asked, even though they knew the answer to that one.

"Yeah. I liked him." Her tone sharpened. "I'm a grown woman, Deputy McBride. I don't need anyone's permission to take a man back to my room."

"Of course not. I wasn't implying—"

"Good. I hope not."

"What else can you tell me about him?" Lucas asked, moving on.

"Well, he was polite and easygoing, and he didn't come on too strong, which, trust me, already puts him ahead of most men in a place like that. He kept the conversation light, didn't pry, didn't try to impress me with whatever he does for a living."

"Did he mention where he was from or what he did?"

"No, and I didn't ask," she replied. "I spend most of my life on the road, Deputy, going from one hotel to the next. When I stop somewhere like that, it's to unwind, not make lasting relationships."

"Gotcha." Lucas made another note, then glanced briefly at Savage before continuing. "Did he seem stressed at all? On edge?"

"No, nothing like that. We had fun."

Savage sighed. Looked like this would be another lead that went nowhere.

"Was he with you the whole time?" Lucas asked. "I mean, he didn't leave your room at any time during the night?"

Her voice was laced with humor. "No, honey. He was with me the *whole* time."

Savage tilted his head. Fair enough.

"Anything else you can tell us about him?" Lucas asked.

She thought for a moment. "He kept himself in good shape for a man his age."

They could see he had a muscular build from the footage.

Lucas finished up. "Okay, thank you, Ms. Baptiste. I think we have everything we need for now."

"Okay, then."

"I appreciate your time."

Lucas ended the call. Turning to Savage he said, "What do you think?"

Savage straightened up, stretching out his back. "I think we need some more information on this mystery man. All we've got is a first name that might not be real and an image on camera. It's not enough to rule him out."

"I could send it to the CBI," Thorpe suggested. "They could run it through facial rec."

Savage gave a reluctant nod. The Colorado Bureau of Investigation was the nearest agency with those kinds of resources. "Yeah, okay. That might be the only shot we have at identifying him."

TWENTY-TWO

SINCLAIR CAME IN AROUND MIDDAY.

"Sorry I'm late," she called as she slumped down in her chair.

"What happened to you?" Lucas asked.

"A lot," she said with emphasis.

Savage came out of his office. She looked pale, and her features were pinched. "You're supposed to be taking it easy. You've got ten stitches in your arm."

"Hard when you have to separate a bunch of brawling teenagers," she muttered.

"What happened?" He walked around her so she wouldn't have to crane her neck to look at him.

"I went to the Wilsons' place, except I put the wrong address into my GPS and ended up on the other side of town in some weird mobile home park. Stupid mistake. I blame the painkillers." She shot an annoyed look at her arm. "Anyway, I was just leaving when I saw two guys going at it in the street. Then two more kids jumped in, and before you know it, they're having a full-on brawl."

"What were they fighting about?"

"A girl."

"A girl?" He raised his eyebrows.

"Yeah. They're sixteen. What else do you fight about when you're sixteen?"

Lucas chuckled.

Thorpe had his earphones on and wasn't listening.

"Anyway, after I broke it up, I drove to the Wilsons' place, for real this time. I spent the last two hours talking to everyone on the street. I had coffee with Bert Manson, you remember him from the Harvest Festival?"

Savage nodded.

"And a slice of apple pie at Mrs. Angelo's. That was the good part." She patted her stomach.

He smirked. "Sounds like quite a morning."

Barb poked her head out of her office. "Dalton, Andre Caldwell called and left a message. He wants you to call him back."

Thorpe took off his headphones and looked around as if noticing everyone for the first time. "Sheriff, I've just heard back from a detective at the CBI."

Savage raised a hand to Barb. "Thanks." He turned to Thorpe. "Go ahead."

"They got no hits on that photograph of our mystery man. Hey, Sinclair. When did you get in?"

"Just now. What mystery man?" she asked.

Savage shook his head, still looking at Thorpe. "Hang on. They got no hits?"

"No, he must not be in any database. It's possible the guy's clean."

"Shit."

"Yep."

"What guy?" Sinclair demanded. "Will someone tell me what's going on?"

Lucas updated her on the man at the casino.

"A hookup?" she asked, arching an eyebrow.

Savage nodded. "Yeah. Could be a credible alibi for a hit man.

He's the right age—late thirties. He'd have been early twenties when the squad was active."

"He was in good shape, too," Lucas added. "According to the witness."

Savage nodded at Lucas to show he agreed. "The hookup, as you put it, could have used the guest to get onto the fifth floor, then snuck out when she fell asleep."

"Did he have a case or bag with him?" Sinclair asked. "Anywhere to hide the hardware?"

"Nope," Lucas admitted. "But that doesn't mean he wasn't carrying a concealed weapon."

She pursed her lips. "Do we have a TOD yet?"

"Actually, I need to chase up on that." Savage swung around and went back to his office. Damned Feds. Info was a one-way street as far as they were concerned.

A frustratingly long phone call later, he had his time of death.

And it wasn't what he'd thought.

"ME puts it between midnight and five in the morning," he said, walking back into the squad room.

"Shit, really?" Sinclair looked up. "That means it could have been any of them."

"Yeah." He gave a tight nod. "Including the mystery man."

THE AFTERNOON WORE ON. Savage sent the crime scene photos he'd taken at the casino to Ray and Pearl, hoping they might find something that would give them a lead.

Since the FBI were being notoriously close-lipped, they'd damn well do their own research. He'd just hit send on the email when there was a knock on the door. He looked up to find Lucas standing there, scratching his head.

"Something bothering you?"

Lucas stepped into the room. "I was just wondering if it would be worth going back to the casino and talking to the dealers and bar staff," he said. "One of them might know Colton, particularly if he's been there before."

"Neither Sam Walking Deer nor Jonas Half Moon recognized him," Savage pointed out.

"I know, but that doesn't mean nobody else will."

Lucas had a point. And since they had nothing else to go on, it was worth a shot.

"Okay, fine," he decided. "But don't be too long. We need you around here."

"Deal." Lucas gave a determined nod before turning and heading back to his desk to grab his keys and badge.

TWENTY-THREE

LUCAS WALKED INTO RIDGEWATER CASINO, but this time he wasn't so overwhelmed by the sudden onslaught of sounds. Slots chimed in the background, cards slapped against felt, and voices carried over the low hum of the room.

He paused inside the entrance and looked around, trying to figure out which table Colton and Renee Baptiste had been playing when they'd met.

He moved toward the blackjack pit, moving with the flow of traffic drifting between tables.

When he got there, he hung back for a few minutes, watching the floor. Dealers rotated in and out, players moved from table to table. Chips clicked in steady rhythm. Drinks were dropped off and left untouched. Nobody looked up unless they had to.

When the dealer paused between hands, Lucas stepped in.

"Got a minute?" He flashed his badge. Someone at the table groaned.

"You gonna shuffle or what?"

The dealer glanced at it, then nodded. "Give me five minutes, then I'm off."

Lucas stepped back again.

When the hand had played out, the shift changed, and the dealer nodded to him. "Sorry, players get angsty if you talk mid-game. So do the pit bosses, and they're always watching."

Lucas nodded. "You working this table the night of November second?"

"Yeah," the guy said. "But we rotate. Everyone does a stretch here."

He could see that. Taking out the still of the mystery man, Lucas handed it to the dealer. "You recognize this guy?"

The dealer studied the photo for a few seconds, then shook his head. "Nah. Doesn't ring a bell. Sorry."

Lucas gave a nod. "Who else was on that night?"

"Best bet is to ask the pit boss." The dealer jerked his chin across the room. "He keeps all the rotation logs."

"Where'll I find him?"

"Over by the craps table."

Lucas followed his line of sight. "Thanks," he said, and moved off, leaving the guy to his break.

The pit boss, a man who wore a permanent frown like he was continually stressed, took Lucas behind the desk.

"We have five dealers on rotation each night," he said, pulling up the shift log on a monitor. He read off the names. "They're on thirty-minute turns."

"I'll need to speak to them," Lucas said.

"What? All of them?"

"Yeah, except for that guy who just clocked off."

The pit boss sighed. "Apart from Clive, only three others are here tonight. Betsy's off sick. Flu," he added, as if it was a huge inconvenience.

"Can you point them out to me?"

The pit boss gave a reluctant nod, then said, "Follow me."

AN HOUR LATER, Lucas strode back into the sheriff's department, triumphant.

"You got it?" Sinclair asked, seeing his face.

"Yep." He held up a piece of paper.

"What'd you find?" Savage asked, coming out of his office.

"The mystery man's name is Colton Reed," Lucas explained, grinning. "He's a pipeline maintenance contractor. Works jobs across southern Colorado and into New Mexico. Been on a crew out near Cortez for the past few weeks."

Savage gave a pleased nod. "Good job. How'd you find that out?"

"One of the dealers remembered him." Lucas took a seat behind his desk. "Said he's seen him a couple of times before. Not a regular, but he passes through when he's working nearby. According to them, he keeps to himself, plays a little blackjack, then moves on."

"Drifter?" Sinclair muttered.

Lucas nodded. "Yeah, and it gets better. I tracked down the crew he's with. They're staying at a motel off Highway 160. Foreman confirmed Reed was working the day of the second, took the night off, but was back on site the following morning. Said his men often go to the Ridgewater to blow off steam."

"High-stress job," Sinclair pointed out.

Savage's expression didn't change. "That doesn't clear him."

"No," Lucas agreed. "But Baptiste's keycard shows she went into the room at eleven thirty-four. No further entries logged until the morning."

Savage's gaze narrowed. "That doesn't mean he stayed put. If he snuck out during the night, he could have propped the door open."

"Renee Baptiste said he didn't leave her bed until the morning," Lucas reminded them. She'd struck him as a smart, confident woman who'd have noticed if her lover had left her hotel room in the middle of the night.

The sheriff let out a low hiss. "Yeah, you're right. Okay, well let's do a background check on Colton Reed and see if he's got any skeletons. If not, I guess he's in the clear too."

Thorpe, who Lucas could see was already logged into the database, ran the name.

"No criminal record. Wasn't in the military. No obvious red flags," his colleague said a moment later without looking up.

Lucas glanced at Savage. "Seems like Colton Reed was just a guy passing through, then. Working a job, blowing off steam."

Silence settled over the room.

Lucas thought his boss looked tired and frustrated, but he couldn't blame him. They were fast running out of suspects.

"Then we're done with him." Savage turned to go back to his office. "Which means we're no closer to finding our killer."

Lucas glanced at the others and shrugged. He was about to get back to work when his cell phone rang. Looking at the number on the screen, he frowned.

"Hello?" he said, picking up.

"Yeah, hello," said a hesitant male voice. "This Deputy McBride?"

"Speaking."

"This is Max Hogarth. I found your card in my front door. I take it you came looking for me?"

Ah, the retired fire chief.

"Yes, that's right. Thanks for calling me back."

He grunted. "What can I help you with, Deputy?"

Lucas got up and walked away from the others. Not so he wasn't overheard, but so he didn't disturb them. Sinclair was concentrating hard on something, and Thorpe was scowling at his computer. Besides, activity always helped him think better.

"I'm interested in a fire that took place out on the Garrity land. The entire family perished, I believe. This would be going back twenty years now. I heard you worked that fire."

There was a long pause. So long, in fact, Lucas thought maybe he'd cut off.

"Sir?"

"Yeah, I'm still here. Who told you I worked that fire?"

"The fire chief here in Hawk's Landing, Mason O'Riley."

"How'd that young gun know?" he muttered.

"He said he'd heard you and some others talking about it once."

"Ah—" He faded off. "Careful what you say, eh?"

"Sir?"

"Yes, I was there. Worst fire of my career. No fireman ever wants to see what we saw that day."

"Could you tell me about it?" Lucas asked. "We could meet—"

"No need, Deputy. We arrived long after the fact. The place was a burnt-out wreck when we got there."

"Oh, I thought you fought the fire?"

"It was too hot to get near. The whole place was alight. Like something out of a nightmare. We used the hoses, of course, but it didn't make a stitch of difference. The family were long gone by that time."

"It must have been very hard," he sympathized.

There was a beat, and then Lucas heard a ragged breath. "Anyway, why you want to know about that?"

"There have been some suggestions that the fire was deliberate," he said carefully. "You got an opinion on that?"

Hogarth hesitated. "Who's been saying it was deliberate?"

"Nobody specific. But since that land is part of the proposal for the data center, we have to look into any suggestion that could affect that."

He gave a low snort. "I see. It's that damned data center. Well, I don't know what to tell you, Deputy. That fire was a result of a leaking gas stove. It was in my report. The forensic company that came to assess it said the same thing."

"I've read the report."

"Then you know. It's all there, just as I said."

Lucas frowned. "Okay, but if we could just meet—"

"I'm afraid that's out of the question. I'm leaving tomorrow for Wisconsin. My daughter lives there with her family. I won't be back for some time."

"What about tonight?" Lucas asked.

Sinclair glanced up and mouthed, "What?"

He shook his head.

"Look, Deputy, I've told you what happened. I've got nothing new to add. It was a long time ago, and my report stands. I'm sorry if that's not what you wanted to hear, but it is what it is. I can't change the facts."

"Of course not! I'm not suggesting—"

"I've got to go."

Max Hogarth hung up the phone.

"Well, that was weird," Lucas said, scratching his head.

"What was?" Sinclair asked.

"That was the former fire chief that Mason said I should speak to, Max Hogarth."

"Oh, yeah. I've met him once or twice. Something of a loner," she said.

"Well, I could have sworn he wasn't telling me the whole truth just now." He glanced at his phone.

"About the Garrity fire?" she asked.

He nodded. "Yeah, he said it was caused by the gas stove, and that his report stands."

Sinclair shrugged. "Maybe that's what happened."

"Yeah, maybe. It's just my aunt was certain—"

"No offense, but your aunt can be pretty impulsive," Sinclair pointed out.

She wasn't wrong there.

He sighed. "Yeah, I know. It was just that he sounded like he didn't want to talk about it. That he was scared, almost."

"Hogarth scared?" She scoffed. "That dude might be in his seventies now, but I swear he's not scared of anything."

Lucas shook his head. There was something off about the phone call. He didn't know what, but he knew something had been bothering the old fireman.

TWENTY-FOUR

A PROTEST outside the town hall over the proposed data center development took up the afternoon. Objectors gathered on the steps and spilled out onto the sidewalk, holding signs that read NO DATA FARM IN OUR VALLEY, SAVE OUR WATER, and JOBS AT WHAT COST?

The crowd was loud without being unruly, voices rising and falling in waves as traffic slowed to a crawl along Main Street. A couple of town hall officials were already there trying to keep things moving, but it was a losing battle. More people kept stopping, drawn in by the noise, talking to protesters, then drifting into the crowd themselves. It was picking up momentum.

Clara McBride stood near the front, impossible to miss, her voice carrying as she spoke to a knot of people gathered around her. A handful of the town's more influential residents stood nearby, lending quiet weight to the whole thing.

Savage recognized most of them. Guardians.

He scowled as he climbed out of his Suburban. "That doesn't bode well."

Sinclair, who had ridden with him, nodded. "The old guard is all here."

The Guardians weren't just another local group. They were landowners and business leaders, people with deep roots in the county, some going back to its origins. They didn't show up like this unless they meant to push back hard.

"If they're involved, this isn't going away anytime soon," Savage muttered, as they started toward the steps.

Conversations dipped as people noticed the officers weaving through the crowd. A few heads turned, a couple of respectful nods in acknowledgment.

Savage spotted Jasmine Hatch halfway up the steps, and a flicker of guilt hit him. He hadn't seen her in months. She stood holding a paper cup, talking to a couple of women, her expression set. Known across town for her coffee, Jasmine was also the mother of Rachel Hatch, a former member of the department, and, for a short time, something more to him.

But Rachel had left Hawk's Landing not long after his first case as sheriff. Life had moved on. He'd met Becca. Built something else. They hadn't kept in touch.

That didn't excuse him not checking in.

Jed Russell stood beside Jasmine, solid and steady as ever. A retired 101st Airborne veteran, he carried himself with the same quiet authority Savage remembered. He'd helped the department once, back when things had turned tactical, and had earned Savage's respect in the process. Around town, people listened when Jed spoke.

Savage slowed as he reached the steps, catching Jasmine's eye. She broke off from her conversation and gave him a warm smile. "Dalton. It's good to see you."

"Jasmine. Didn't expect to see you here." She lived outside of town on a sprawling property near the foothills, and usually only came in once or twice a week for supplies.

She nodded to the signs, then back at him. "Figured I should be. This matters to me."

"Yeah. Seems like it matters to a lot of people."

There was a brief pause.

"You've been keeping busy," she said. "Haven't seen you in a while."

"I know. I'm sorry, I've been meaning to stop by. We're overdue a catchup, and I miss your famous brew."

That earned a faint smile. "You're always welcome."

"I'll come by," he promised. "Soon."

"I'll look forward to it," she replied, smiling.

Standing near the top of the steps, Clara McBride caught his eye.

"Excuse me," he said, nodding to Jasmine and moving toward Clara. She stood firm, defiance in her stance. Thankfully, she didn't have her shotgun with her today.

"Sheriff," she said, as he approached.

"Clara." He glanced around at the crowd. "I hope you're planning on keeping this under control."

"It is under control," she said evenly. "Peaceful protest. We're just exercising our rights as citizens."

Savage looked past her at the swelling crowd, the traffic backing up along Main.

"You're blocking half the street."

"They can go around." She folded her arms. "Nobody's breaking the law."

She was right. Unless it turned violent, there was nothing they could do.

"Just make sure it stays that way."

Before Clara could respond, a black SUV pulled up hard at the opposite curb. The driver's door swung open and Mayor Jasper "J.J." McAllister stepped out, already flushed and irritated.

"This'll be fun," Clara smirked and nodded at the furious-looking mayor.

"I'll take care of it," Savage said, moving off to intercept him.

"This is out of order," McAllister said, reaching Savage at the edge of the crowd. "Completely out of order."

Savage turned to face him. "Afternoon, Mayor."

McAllister barely acknowledged him, his attention fixed on the crowd. "You need to move them on, Sheriff. They're blocking public access to a municipal building."

"They're within their rights," he said evenly.

"That's not what it looks like to me."

The front doors of the town hall opened, and Nancy Monroe stepped out onto the top step. Svelte and smartly dressed, she looked like she meant business.

"Oh, boy," murmured Sinclair, who'd joined him. "Here we go."

Monroe paused, taking in the scene, her expression tightening as her gaze settled on Clara. For a moment, the two women simply stared at each other. Then Monroe descended the steps with measured calm and joined Savage, Sinclair, and the mayor, bypassing Clara completely.

A strategic move. She was remaining neutral.

"Sheriff, Deputy," she greeted them. "Mayor."

"Councilwoman," Savage replied.

McAllister gave a quick nod and waved his hand at the crowd like they were pesky mosquitoes. "We can't have this kind of disruption every time someone disagrees with a proposal."

Monroe didn't respond immediately. Turning, she surveyed the protesters, the signs, the people gathered there.

"People are entitled to make their views known," she said, facing him again.

"That's one way of putting it," McAllister muttered.

Monroe's expression remained neutral, but Savage caught something in it. Not approval exactly, but not annoyance either. Could it be that she wasn't a fan of the development either?

"As long as it remains peaceful, there's no reason for intervention," she said to Savage.

He nodded. "That's how I see it."

Clara was talking to Jasmine now. Savage hadn't realized they knew each other. The way Jasmine had her hand on Clara's arm, they were definitely friends.

"Excuse me." Monroe gave a small, polite nod and headed back up the steps, stopping to talk to other people on the way. Always on show, always the politician.

Sinclair tapped Savage on the shoulder, and he turned away from McAllister, grateful for the distraction. She pointed to a young teenage couple near the sidewalk. "See that kid over there?"

Savage followed her gaze. "Yeah."

"He's one of the brawlers from the other day. You know, the fight I broke up on Maple Ridge Street."

Savage frowned. "Oh, yeah."

She let out a short laugh. "Looks like he got the girl."

"Maple Ridge? I thought you got the address wrong?"

She glanced at him. "I did. Put in Maple Ridge Street instead of Lane. That's why I ended up on the wrong side of town. They're in completely different districts."

"Maple Ridge Street," he repeated.

Sinclair shrugged. "Yeah. Wilsons are on Lane. I was miles off."

Savage glanced back toward the crowd, but he wasn't seeing it anymore.

TWENTY-FIVE

SAVAGE WAS quiet all the way back to the department. They'd left two security guards from a company assigned to protect the mayor —much to McAllister's annoyance—to oversee the protest. If it escalated at all, they were to give him a call.

"You okay?" Sinclair asked, glancing over at him.

"Yeah, just thinking."

She nodded, and bit her lip, staring out the windshield as they rode the short distance back to the office. He appreciated that she gave him space. Over the last few years, they'd learned to read each other pretty well. He, Sinclair, and Thorpe were a tight unit. Lucas was getting there. Together, they made a great team.

He wondered what they'd think of his theory.

"Okay, listen up," he said when they got back.

Lucas turned in his chair. Thorpe slid off his headphones. Sinclair frowned but didn't speak as she took her seat.

In the front office, Barb reached over and turned down the radio. She didn't come in, but Savage knew she was listening.

"The mix-up with the streets," he began, looking at Sinclair. "It got me thinking. We might be looking at this whole case the wrong way."

Thorpe frowned. "What do you mean?"

"The original victims, Frank and Sarah Wilson… They lived on Maple Ridge Lane, right?"

Thorpe nodded.

Sinclair's eyes widened as she began to see where he was going with this. "Yeah, but there are *two* Maple Ridges in Hawk's Landing. I told you, I put Maple Ridge Street into my GPS yesterday and ended up on the opposite side of town."

Lucas had gone still now, watching Savage closely. Thorpe's expression sharpened.

"What if," Savage said softly, "the killer made the same mistake?"

No one spoke for a long moment.

Sinclair blinked, then shook her head, like she was trying to push the thought away. "You think Frank and Sarah were *not* the intended targets?"

Savage shrugged but didn't reply. He wanted them to sit with it for a while, as he had done, churning it over in their minds.

The pause dragged out.

Lucas shifted in his chair. "It's possible," he said finally, breaking the silence. "I didn't even know there were two roads with that name."

"Small difference," Thorpe amended. "But an easy enough mistake to make."

Barb stepped into the doorway now, her arms folded. Savage looked up at her.

"If that's true," her voice was a strained whisper, "then they died for nothing."

He gave a grim nod.

Thorpe removed his glasses and set them carefully on his desk. "Then the question is… who was the original target?" He looked at each of them in turn. "Who lives at forty-six Maple Ridge Street?"

Slowly, all eyes turned to Sinclair.

She froze for a second, then swallowed as she realized what was at stake.

"I—I don't know. I didn't stop. I realized I was in the wrong place, broke up the scuffle, and left." She dragged a hand through her hair. "I didn't even think to check who lived at number forty-six."

"You couldn't have known," Lucas said.

"It didn't even occur to me," she murmured, rubbing at the bandage on her arm.

"It's not your fault," Savage grunted, crossing his arms over his chest. "None of us made the connection. I didn't know there were two roads called that either."

"I should have," Sinclair insisted. "I'm from here, goddamnit."

"Still, you can't know every road in the place," Barb reasoned. "Besides, I grew up here and I didn't even know."

Sinclair flattened her lips but gave an annoyed nod.

Thorpe turned back to his keyboard and ran a couple of commands. They all knew he was pulling the address through the county property register.

The room fell quiet except for the steady clatter of keys.

"Come on..." he muttered.

A few seconds passed.

Then he frowned.

"That's odd."

Savage stepped closer. "What?"

Thorpe leaned back slightly, eyes still scanning. "Forty-six Maple Ridge Street doesn't have any data attached. There is no current tax record and no listed owner." He clicked again. "Last update was, well, never."

Lucas frowned. "That doesn't make sense. Someone's got to live there."

"They probably do," Thorpe said. "But not in any way the system recognizes."

"It was a strange place," Sinclair said, frowning. "There were a bunch of prefab units, mobile homes, even some trailers."

Thorpe pulled up a Google maps and zoomed in.

"See this?" He gestured at the screen. They crowded around. "This whole stretch is not laid out like a normal street. Looks like it was one parcel that got carved up over time. No formal re-registration."

Sinclair leaned in. "That does make sense."

Thorpe nodded. "Zones like this fall through the cracks, especially if people are renting space informally or paying cash for units."

"Then there are no deeds?" Savage asked.

"Maybe for the land," Thorpe said, frowning. "I'll look into who owns the whole thing, but not for what's sitting on it. Doesn't look like any units on that property have ever been registered."

Savage felt a tightening in his chest. "So 'forty-six' might not even officially exist."

"Exactly."

A beat.

"Meaning," Savage said, "we don't know who lives there."

Thorpe shook his head. "Not from this."

Savage made a quick decision. "We're not waiting on paperwork. I'm going to head out there now."

Lucas was already pushing his chair back. "I'm in."

Sinclair grabbed her jacket, forgetting about her injured arm. "Let's go."

Savage looked back at Thorpe. "Stay on it. I want everything you can scrape together on that property. Old records, utility hookups, anything. We need to find out who owns it."

Thorpe nodded, already turning back to the screen.

"Call me the second you get something."

Savage headed for the door, Lucas and Sinclair right behind him.

TWENTY-SIX

IT TOOK LONGER than usual to cut across town on account of the ongoing protest. Traffic was backed up three blocks from Main, horns blaring, people spilling off sidewalks into the road. Savage swore under his breath and swung the wheel hard, cutting down a side street to loop around. Lucas, who followed in the cruiser, did the same.

By the time they cleared the congestion, the town had thinned out. Storefronts gave way to empty lots, chain-link fences, and low industrial buildings with sun-faded signage. The road narrowed as the asphalt turned rough and patchy, the edges crumbling into dirt.

"Not much of a street at all," Sinclair murmured.

Savage slowed as they turned in, scanning the immediate area. What should have been a neat run of houses was anything but.

The land spread unevenly on either side, dotted with mobile homes in various states of repair. Some had sagging steps and patched siding, while others were surprisingly neat with potted plants and swept gravel.

Camper vans sat wedged between them, a few on blocks, one with a blue tarp stretched over the roof. Powerlines drooped low overhead, cables branching off in ways that didn't look entirely official.

Off to the left, two long, derelict warehouse buildings loomed, their windows boarded or broken, graffiti sprawled across the brickwork. Around it, a rusted chain-link fence leaned inward as if it had given up trying to stand straight.

He brought the Suburban to a stop and cut the engine. Lucas pulled up beside him, and they all climbed out.

"That's thirty-two," he said, as a number on a mailbox caught his eye.

Sinclair scoffed and pointed ahead. "That one says fifty."

He let out a frustrated breath. "There's no order to it."

No consistent spacing or reliable numbering. Some places did have numbers stenciled on the door, others had scribbles on mailboxes, but plenty had nothing at all.

A couple of residents lingered outside, watching them climb out of the SUV with guarded curiosity.

"Evening," Savage called, nodding at them.

He got one or two nods in return.

"Not the most welcoming of places," Sinclair murmured.

"Okay, let's spread out and look for number forty-six," Savage said, turning to face them. "Remember, this isn't an ideal layout. There are blind spots between the trailers, narrow gaps, the warehouses at the back."

They both nodded.

"I'll take the right side," Lucas said, gesturing in that direction. "I'll work toward the warehouses."

Savage nodded. "Sinclair, you're with me. We start left and move in. Keep your eyes peeled."

She placed her hand on her holster. "Ready when you are."

They spread out.

About fifty yards down, Savage spotted a man working in his front yard. He was carrying a heavy-looking potted plant.

"Afternoon," he called. Sinclair followed behind him, watching his six.

The guy was in his fifties, slim but lithe, and wore a Colorado Rockies baseball cap. He gave a nod.

"Mind telling me which one is number forty-six?" Savage asked.

The man set the plant down with a grunt, then straightened. "Hard to tell, I know, but it's that unit over there, behind the tree." He nodded toward it.

Savage thanked him and headed over to what was definitely a modular home. It appeared to have been built in sections and on-site, but it had a permanent foundation and was more house-like than trailer.

Sinclair beckoned to Lucas, and they fanned out behind him.

Up close, the place looked lived-in but tired. Faded siding, patched in places. A couple of plastic chairs sat by the door, one cracked down the middle. Wind chimes rattled softly in the breeze, out of tune.

Savage knocked.

There was movement inside. A pause. Then the door opened.

A man in his early sixties stood there, broad-shouldered but softened with age. Close-cropped gray hair, weathered skin. He looked between them. "Can I help you?"

"Afternoon," Savage said. "Sheriff's department. Mind if we have a word?"

The man hesitated, then stepped back, opening the door wider. "Yeah, sure. Come on in."

Savage gave a small nod as they stepped inside. "What is your name, sir?"

"Ed Burges. But my friends call me Buddy."

"Appreciate it, Buddy. This is just a routine inquiry. We had a bit of unrest in the area the other day and wanted to check in with folks nearby."

Buddy gave a soft snort. "Yeah, I heard something about that.

Doesn't surprise me." He gestured vaguely around. "Place ain't what it used to be."

"You've lived here a while?" Savage asked as they followed him into the living room.

"Long enough," Buddy said, pointing to the sofa and a worn armchair. "Used to be decent. Good people, looked out for each other. Last ten years..." He shook his head. "Gone downhill. All kinds of people moved in. Now it's the kind of place folks drive around, not through."

Savage glanced around the room as they spoke. Nobody sat down. It was sparse but tidy. A small TV stood in the corner on a console table. The couch and armchair were at least a couple decades old. A coffee table stood in the center, piled with a stack of newspapers and magazines.

On the wall, he noticed a couple of framed photos. And on a shelf, military memorabilia. A folded flag in a case. A couple of patches. A plaque.

Lucas caught his eye and gave a small nudge in that direction.

Savage nodded to the shelf. "You served?"

Buddy followed his gaze, then gave a small shrug. "Yeah. Long time ago now."

"What unit?" Savage asked, casual.

"Army," Buddy said. "10th Mountain Division. Spent some time overseas back in the day."

"You stay in after that?" Lucas asked.

"Nah," Buddy said. "Did some contract security work for a bit. Desk job mostly. Nothing worth writing home about." He gave a faint smile. "Then came out here with my late wife, God rest her soul. Worked in insurance for the last fifteen years."

"Sorry to have to ask, but can you remember where you were on the evening of November second?"

Buddy scratched his head. "Now you're asking. I was either here or at the Spur. That's a bar not too far away. A group of us old-timers get together every Friday night and have a few beers."

"This was a Thursday night," Savage said.

A shrug. "Oh, well, then I was probably here. Don't go much anyplace else."

"Anyone vouch for you?"

He glanced at Savage. "The way you say that anyone would think I was a suspect or something, Sheriff. As I recall, that unrest you were talking happened a couple days ago, not last week."

He was smart, Savage gave him that much.

"It's a related incident," he lied.

"Well, I keep to myself," he said evenly. "My truck was in the driveway. If any of the neighbors saw it, they could tell you that."

"That's something," Savage said with a nod.

Nothing in the man's tone suggested he was lying. No hesitation. No flicker of pretense. Buddy seemed like your average guy who'd served for a while, then ended up here.

Savage stepped back toward the door.

"Well, we won't take up any more of your time. Thanks for talking with us."

"Oh, one last thing," Lucas said, as they were about to leave.

"Yeah?" Buddy stopped in the hallway.

"You ever hear of a unit called Department Nine when you were serving?"

Buddy frowned, confusion crossing his face. "Can't say I did."

Lucas met Savage's gaze and gave a shrug.

Savage forced a smile. "Thanks again."

"No problem. You folks stay safe out there."

They stepped outside, the door closing behind them.

"What do you think?" Savage asked, once they were clear of the porch.

There was a momentary pause. The breeze stirred loose dust along the cracked asphalt, rattling a sheet of tin on one of the nearby trailers. Somewhere in the distance, a dog barked, then fell silent again.

"He seemed genuine to me," Sinclair said, frowning as she

glanced back at the double-wide. “I can’t see why he’d be a target any more than the Wilsons.”

“He was in the army, at least.” Lucas nodded toward the house. “There could be something there. Old connection, maybe.”

“I’m not sure.” Savage scanned up and down the street again, his gaze lingering on the mismatched trailers, the rusted-out vehicles, the gaps where properties didn’t seem to follow any kind of order. “He didn’t appear to know anything about the unit.”

“Are we sure the killer made a mistake?” Sinclair asked, shoving her hands into her jacket pockets.

“No, we’re not sure of anything,” Savage said, brusquer than he’d meant. He softened his tone. “That’s why we’re here. Checking it out.”

“Well, the house numbers don’t help,” Lucas pointed out. “Even if the killer had got the street right, I doubt he’d have found the property.”

Sinclair threw up her hands. “Half these places don’t even have numbers. And the ones that do are all over the place. Odds, evens, some missing altogether. How the hell does the postal service find anyone?”

That was a good question.

Savage let out a slow breath. “When we get back, we dig into Ed Burges. We scrutinize everything. His service record, work history, anyone he’s crossed paths with. Anything that might’ve put him on someone’s radar.”

Sinclair nodded. “I’ll radio Thorpe on the way back.”

“Lucas, you mind staying and talking to some of the residents? Find out if they’ve noticed anything strange lately, what they think of Buddy over there. You know the drill.”

Lucas gave a nod and headed off.

Savage got back into the Suburban and waited for Sinclair to climb into the passenger seat. Then he pulled out, tires kicking up gravel as they went.

As they left, Savage glanced in the rearview mirror. Ed Burges’s house was so set back from the road and nestled behind the trees that he could hardly see it.

The guy had appeared innocent enough, but Savage's gut was telling him he wasn't wrong. That this was the right street. He just didn't know why the man in that house had been picked.

The other, more ominous thought that crossed his mind as he drove back to the department was—if Buddy had been the original target, who's to say whoever wanted him dead wouldn't try again?

TWENTY-SEVEN

IT WAS dark by the time Savage and Sinclair got back to the department.

"You want coffee?" she asked, heading for the breakroom.

"No, thanks."

He went to his office and closed the door. It was time to make a phone call. There was one person who might know whether Ed Burges had anything to do with Department Nine, and that was the retired CIA analyst, Edgar Zales.

So far, Zales seemed to be the only one who knew anything about the unit at all. If it hadn't been for the heavily redacted files, and the names he'd been given, Savage would question whether it really existed.

Zales' number was already in his recent calls. Taking a seat, he hit the call button and lifted the phone to his ear. It rang a couple of times, but the analyst didn't answer. On the fourth ring, it clicked over to voicemail.

Savage hated leaving messages on machines, but this was important. Still, he hesitated for a fraction of a second before he spoke.

"This is Sheriff Savage. Give me a call when you get this. Got a question for you." He ended the call without elaborating. No point putting anything sensitive on a recording.

For a second, he remained where he was, phone still in hand, as if expecting it to ring straight back. When it didn't, he slipped it into his pocket and pushed himself away from the desk.

That's when he saw the sticky note in Barb's neat handwriting.

Call Andre Caldwell. Beneath it, she'd scribbled a number.

He stuck it in his pocket. Barb had already left, but Thorpe was still at his desk, while Sinclair was nursing her coffee and reading something on her computer screen.

"You had a break today?" Savage asked Thorpe, who appeared even more disheveled than he'd been earlier.

His deputy took off his glasses and rubbed his eyes. There were deep imprints on either side of his nose. "I'm fine."

He didn't look it.

"I want you to go home," Savage said firmly. "Burges can wait until tomorrow."

"I've dug up everything I can find on the guy already," Thorpe said, nodding to Sinclair.

"Everything he said checks out," she told Savage, swinging around to face him. "Wife, insurance company, even his military stretch. Two tours. Opted out after that. Clean discharge."

"Any special forces training?" he asked.

"Nothing," Thorpe replied.

Savage walked over to the crime board and stared at the list of names. "He's not one of these guys?"

"Nope. Not from what I can see," Thorpe said. "I'm cross-referencing on every system I have access to. And some I don't," he murmured, under his breath.

Savage ignored that last part.

"There has to be some kind of connection," he rubbed his forehead. Tension and tiredness were giving him a headache. They all needed a break. "Why else would he have been targeted?"

"We don't know that he was," Sinclair said from behind them.

Savage gave a grunt of acknowledgement. "But it makes a damn sight more sense than the Wilsons."

"What happened to his wife?" Savage asked, turning around.

"She died in a jet ski accident on holiday in the Bahamas," Thorpe told him. "She'd gone down there with some friends. Doesn't look like Ed was with her at the time."

Savage frowned. "Anything unusual about her death?"

"Nope. Bunch of kids misbehaving on their parents' boat. Didn't see her until it was too late. She died of impact wounds on the way to hospital."

"That's just awful," Sinclair said.

Savage rubbed a hand over his face, the stubble rough against his palm. "When exactly did she die?"

"Seven years ago."

Savage was quiet for a moment, processing. Then he said, "Well, I've got to admit, that doesn't sound suspicious to me."

"Poor guy," Sinclair murmured.

"I'll keep digging," Thorpe was already turning back to his screen. "If I find anything, I'll let you know."

"No. You've done enough for one day. Pack up and get home. We can pick this up tomorrow."

"You sure—"

"I'm sure," Savage cut in, as Lucas walked in.

"Find anything interesting?" he asked Lucas, who shook his head.

"Not much. Nobody likes to pry, it turns out. Some of those people don't even know who lives one door down."

Savage snorted. "Okay, thanks for trying."

The main office phone rang. Sinclair answered, since Barb had already left for the day.

"It's a Detective Wexford from Denver PD on the phone. Says he wants to speak with you."

He frowned. "Wexford? Don't know him."

Sinclair shrugged. "Well, he's on Line 1."

Savage went back to his office to take the call.

"Savage," he barked into the desk phone.

"Sheriff Savage?"

"Yeah. How can I help you?"

"Detective Wexford from Denver PD. We got your number off Edgar Zales' answering machine."

Savage felt a sinking feeling in his gut. "Everything okay?"

"No, Sheriff. Afraid not. Edgar Zales was killed in a hit-and-run this morning."

Savage sank down into his chair. "What happened?"

Wexford had a typical law enforcement tone. Even, controlled, just stating the facts. "He was crossing a street. Truck came out of nowhere. Witnesses said it jumped a red light, hit him, and kept going."

Savage closed his eyes. *Fuck.*

"You get a plate?" he rasped. He'd really liked the old guy.

"No. Camera blind spot. Witnesses didn't get a good enough look at the vehicle. All they could tell me was that it was black and dirty."

Savage clenched his jaw, pressing the phone to his ear. He was willing to bet the plate was stolen anyway. Or concealed with dirt.

"If you don't mind me asking, what was your business with Edgar Zales?" Wexford inquired.

Savage chose his words carefully. "He was helping me with a case. A double homicide here in La Plata County. I'm afraid I can't say more than that."

There was a pause.

"You think your investigation had anything to do with his death?" Wexford asked.

Savage let out a breath. More to force himself to sound normal than anything else. He didn't want Wexford to know how angry he was. "Don't think so. The person of interest was someone Zales was looking into twenty years ago. Doubt he's still around."

That much was partially true, at least.

Gregory wasn't.

The rest of it... he wasn't so sure.

"All right," Wexford said. "Appreciate your time. Good luck with your case."

"You too," Savage said. Then lower, "I hope you find the bastard who did this."

"Yeah. Me too. Scumbag shouldn't be allowed to get away with it."

He wouldn't. Savage promised himself that much. When he found the bastard, he would make him pay. For the Wilsons. For Zales.

For the fucking inconvenience.

Savage said goodbye, and the line clicked dead.

Wexford would never find the driver of that truck, because that had been a deliberate hit made to look like an accident. Someone had known Zales had talked. That he had information that could help find the killer. And they wanted to stop him from saying anything else.

Slowly, feeling like he was a hundred years old, Savage got to his feet. Whatever Zales had known had just died with him. All they had now was the folder the CIA agent had given them and the names on the slip of paper tucked inside.

With a heavy heart, Savage went to tell the others what had happened.

TWENTY-EIGHT

THORPE HAD JUST SWUNG his backpack onto his back when Savage marched back into the squad room. "What's up?" he said, immediately.

Both Sinclair and Lucas glanced up.

"Edgar Zales is dead."

"What?" Sinclair blurted.

"Isn't he the guy that gave you the folder?" Lucas asked, frowning.

Thorpe sank back down into his chair, backpack still on his back.

Savage tried to keep his voice steady, but it was tough. The old guy had done nothing but help them. He didn't deserve this.

"Yeah. Hit-and-run. Don't believe it for a second." Not anymore. Not after everything that had happened.

"It could be a horrible coincidence." Sinclair stared at him. He knew she was just trying to rationalize it, but there was no rationalizing this. The people, or person, pulling the strings were not rational.

"You really think that?"

She held his gaze for a moment, then shook her head. "Not really."

"How did they know?" Lucas asked.

"They must have been keeping tabs on him," Savage muttered.

"Or us," Thorpe added.

Savage considered this, balling his hands into fists. That was the more likely scenario. They were the ones leading the investigation into the homicides. *He* was the one who'd contacted Zales, which meant the former analyst was dead because of him.

A long beat passed where nobody said anything. Thorpe removed his pack and leaned back in his chair. Lucas was like a statue, while Sinclair had her hand over her mouth.

He knew he had to lead the discussion here, but he was so mad, he could barely think straight. Taking a deep breath, he forced himself to relax.

"Okay, let's think about this logically," he said, looking at each of them individually, but the words were directed at himself. "We know Gregory killed the Wilsons. He used the same bullets, had the same shoe size. It all points to him."

"But that was a mistake," Sinclair whispered through her splayed fingers.

Savage inclined his head. "Let's assume he meant to kill Ed Burges and got the address wrong."

"Then someone killed him," Lucas said. "Could it have been Burges?"

Thorpe straightened. "Actually, that makes sense. If Burges heard about the hit and realized he was the intended target, he could have gone after Gregory to neutralize the threat."

Lucas gave a nod. "They could've been in the same unit."

"Burges is much older than Gregory," Savage pointed out.

"Fifteen years, give or take," Lucas replied. "That's not a deal-breaker. I've seen guys in their late thirties being pulled into specialist units. Burges could've been more experienced when he was recruited."

"He'd left the military by then," Thorpe said, shaking his head. "It can't be him."

"Unless that insurance story is fake?" Sinclair raised her eyebrows.

Thorpe shrugged. "I'll look into it some more just to be sure, but it didn't appear to be."

"If Burges shot Gregory at the casino, how'd he get to him?" Savage asked. "He wasn't on the fifth floor, or we would've seen him. If he was staying at the hotel, he'd be on the guest register."

Sinclair shook her head. "You're right. He couldn't have."

"We've been through every guest," Lucas said, shoulders dropping. "I checked them out myself. Burges wasn't there."

Yet somebody shot Gregory.

It felt like they were chasing their goddamn tails.

"You know what," Savage heaved a sigh. "Let's call it a night. Get some rest. Think it over. We'll regroup in the morning."

"Who's on call?" Thorpe asked.

"I am." Sinclair held up her phone.

Savage didn't insist they stay at the office when on call, not unless they had a suspect in custody. The main line would route through to their cells. That way, they could have a life outside of work and wouldn't miss sleep unnecessarily.

If for some reason the deputy didn't respond, the call would divert to all their phones. Either way, they were covered.

SAVAGE WANTED nothing more than to sit on his porch with a beer, watch the stars come out, and talk to Becca. It would be too late to catch Connor before his bedtime, but he could still speak to her. Maybe she'd be in a talking mood tonight.

It was times like this that he missed her more than ever. He remembered how they used to sit at the kitchen table and pick apart a case. She'd help him unmuddle his thoughts, see things clearly.

There was this way about her, a rational logic honed from years as a psychologist that he just didn't have. But it was more than that. He missed her presence, her sense of humor, the way her eyes lit up when she smiled. Becca understood him. She saw right through the gruff exterior and straight into his soul.

Damn.

He forwent the beer and sat on the porch instead, pulling out his phone. It was a clear, cloudless night. The sky had turned a deep indigo to the east, fading to a lighter shade in the west, still tinged with orange.

The hills loomed ahead, dark purple silhouettes still healing from the wildfires that had nearly destroyed the national forest. Even now, in the dim light, he could make out the scorched scars along the ridge.

He dialed Becca's number.

It rang four, maybe five times. He was about to hang up when she answered. She sounded breathy, like she'd been rushing.

"Hey, you okay?" he asked.

"Hi. Yeah, I'm fine."

"This a bad time?"

"Actually, yeah. I'm about to go out."

He frowned. It was late for an excursion.

"Where you guys going?"

There was a pause.

"Not us, just me. Connor's here, with the babysitter."

"I see."

There was an edge to her voice. "I have a life too, you know, Dalton."

"Of course." He steered the conversation back to his son. "Is Connor asleep? Can I see him?"

"He's asleep. I'd rather not disturb him."

"You sure everything's all right?" A cold chill slid up the back of his neck that had nothing to do with the night air.

"Listen, Dalton. I've been meaning to talk to you about something."

He sat very still. "Yeah?"

"This isn't easy for me to say, but… I'm seeing someone."

His chest constricted, and for a moment, he couldn't speak. Couldn't even draw breath. It felt like all the air had been knocked out of him in one go.

"Dalton, you there?"

He sucked in a breath. "Yeah."

"Did you hear me?"

"I heard you."

What did she expect him to say? That he was okay with it? That he hoped she had a good time? That he didn't mind her being with someone else?

Christ.

"I'm sorry. I know this must be a shock."

He couldn't find the words. Something twisted inside. He wanted to tell her not to go. To tell her she was making a mistake. That they could fix this, if she'd just give them another chance. But none of it came out.

He just sat there in the dark, the only sound his heart hammering in his ears.

"Dalton… say something."

"What do you want me to say?" The words came out cold. Bitter.

The shock was already giving way to anger.

How could she do this? To him.

To them.

Didn't what they had mean anything?

"I don't know. Something."

He drew in a slow breath, trying to steady himself, to push down the tightness in his chest. "Give Connor my love."

A pause.

"That's it? That's all you've got?"

"It's all I can say. Goodbye, Becca."

He ended the call before she could reply.

Then he went and got a beer.

TWENTY-NINE

SAVAGE WOKE up on the couch and groaned. Jesus, his head hurt.

Turning, he looked at the time on his phone.

Shit.

It was nearly nine o'clock. He was late for work.

He messaged Barb. *On my way. Got held up.*

She texted him a thumbs up emoji in response.

Holding his head, he eased himself off the couch and made his way to the bathroom. He couldn't remember when he last had a hangover. Certainly not one this bad.

Somehow, he managed to shower and get himself dressed, then made a flask of coffee. As he left the house, the pain from Becca's words hit him afresh, but he pushed them aside and forced himself to think about the case. He'd done enough wallowing last night.

Now, he had a murder to solve.

He parked and hurried across the street to the department, only to get intercepted by Councilwoman Monroe as he entered the building.

"Sheriff, can I have a word?"

Dressed in a navy pin-stripe skirt and blazer, she looked every bit the confident and capable councilor she professed to be.

He stopped, turned to face her, and winced as the sun hit his eyes.

"Councilwoman, this is a surprise."

"I wish I could say it was a pleasant one," she said, with a rare smile. "But I have something important to discuss with you."

If they had to do this now...

"I was about to go to my office. Won't you come inside?"

She glanced up and down the street. "I'd rather talk out here."

He frowned. Where they couldn't be overheard? "Okay."

"I received an anonymous letter yesterday," she went on, "and I was wondering if you could tell me who sent it."

"How should I know?"

"It's handwritten, for one. And it concerns the land earmarked for the data center. Specifically, how it was acquired."

"Ah." He nodded slowly. "You think Clara McBride sent it?"

"I don't know who sent it." She reached into her blazer pocket and handed him a folded sheet of paper. "That's why I'm here."

He unfolded it and glanced down. The handwriting was a jerky, uneven printed scrawl, the lines of text sloping noticeably downwards to the right.

"It's not Clara's," he said after a beat. "I can tell you that much."

"Read it," Monroe encouraged.

He scanned the page.

DEAR COUNCILWOMAN MONROE,

Before you sign off on that land, you need to know what happened there.

It wasn't bought fair. People died on that property. Murdered.

I was there. I saw it happen.

You want to build on that land, that's your business. But don't do it without knowing what it cost.

. . .

THERE WAS NO SIGNATURE.

Savage looked up to find her watching him closely.

"Do you know what it means?" she asked.

He hesitated, trying to decide how much to reveal. He didn't want to break Clara's trust, but her accusations were serious. "I might have an idea."

Her eyebrow slanted. "You mind telling me?"

He nodded toward the station door. "You sure you don't want to come inside?"

"I've only got a minute." She gestured toward a black Mercedes idling across the street, driver behind the wheel.

He handed the letter back to her, lowering his voice. "That land was once owned by the Garrity family. Couple hundred acres. This is going back twenty years or so."

She listened without interrupting.

"One night, there was a fire. The ranch house burned to the ground, the family along with it. Husband, wife, and their two young kids died."

She shook her head, then frowned. "The letter says they were murdered."

"I heard the same thing," Savage said. "Rumors, mostly. My deputy's been digging into it. Spoke to Clara McBride. She knew the family. She never bought the official story."

Monroe pursed her lips, thinking.

"Why do you think this was sent to me?" she said, after a beat.

"My guess is that whoever sent that letter wants to stall the vote."

She was silent for a second time.

"I got the impression that the person who wrote it was more concerned with the fire than any development," she said.

She was sharp and had good instincts. "Could be they wanted you to think that."

Her gaze narrowed. “You know who sent it, don’t you?”

“No, I don’t,” he admitted, “But my guess is it was a member of the Guardians. You’ve heard of them, I presume?”

She gave a wry smile. “Ah, yes. The old boys’ network.”

He dipped his head. “That’s one way of putting it.”

“You think they’re trying to pressure me into calling off the vote?” She tapped the folded letter lightly against her palm.

“Wouldn’t be the first time they’ve tried to manipulate an outcome. Listen, I’m sorry, but I really have to get to work. I’m in the middle of a double homicide investigation.”

“I heard. How’s it coming on?”

“We’re making progress,” he lied.

“All right. When you catch your killer”—she slipped the letter back into her blazer pocket—“I’d like you to look into that fire for me. I need to know what I’m dealing with before I take a position.”

Savage gave a small nod. “I’ll do that, Councilor.”

She stepped back toward the curb. “Good luck, Sheriff.”

“Thanks.”

She turned and walked back across the street to where her car was waiting.

Frowning, he opened the door and went inside.

“What did Nancy Monroe want?” Barb asked, as he came in and shot her a good morning nod.

“Wants us to do some digging into the land earmarked for the proposed data center.” He didn’t go into detail. Mostly because his head was killing him and he needed a glass of water and a painkiller. “Told her we’d get to it after we tied up this case.”

She frowned. “Are you all right? You look terrible.”

Was it that obvious?

“I’m fine.” He walked past her into the squad room.

“Andre Caldwell phoned again,” she called after him.

Shit, he’d forgotten to call him back.

“Any update on Ed Burges?” he asked the team, all of whom were already working hard, eyes glued to their screens.

Thorpe removed his earbuds. "The insurance company checked out. His former boss said he'd been a model employee. Took early retirement at sixty, and that's the last they heard of him."

"It can't be him," Sinclair said.

Savage turned to the board. "Okay, so if it's not Burges, it's got to be someone else. One of these men." He poked the list of eight names with his finger.

"I looked into Benjamin Vance, that senior Agency officer Zales mentioned," Thorpe said. "According to Zales's notes, he was the one who sanctioned the investigation into Department Nine, then withdrew it when it was shut down."

"Did you find him?" Savage asked.

"Yes and no. He retired shortly after the unit shut down, but then he and his wife disappeared. The colleague I spoke to said he thought they'd gone to Mexico."

"Mexico?" Savage frowned. "That's quite extreme, isn't it?"

"It's popular with retirees," Thorpe said. "But the interesting thing is there's no forwarding address on any system for him. It's like he up and vanished when he crossed the border."

Lucas glanced up. "Didn't want to be found?"

"Strange for a former State Department official," Savage mused. "Pretty important position."

"He was only there for a couple of years," Thorpe pointed out. "His tenure was marred with controversy. In the end, he was forced out."

"For what?" Savage frowned.

"There was a leak. Classified material. According to an internal review at the time, it was never proven it was him, but it happened on his watch."

"That's all it takes," Sinclair muttered.

"So, we don't know where he is?" Savage rubbed his jaw, even more stubbly than before. He'd forgotten to shave again.

"Could be anywhere," Thorpe said.

"What about the wife? Any way of tracing him through her family?"

"That's what I'm doing now," he said with a backwards nod at his computer.

"Keep me posted," Savage said, jutting out his jaw. "He might know something about Department Nine. We've got to find him."

"If he's still alive," Sinclair pointed out. "It's been twenty years."

"He left at fifty-seven," Thorpe said. "There's a good chance he's still around."

Savage motioned to the board. "Vance aside, we still need to figure out which of these men killed Gregory."

Lucas shook his head. "They could be anyone."

"Could be Burges," Savage said.

"Literally anyone," Lucas repeated, and turned back to his screen.

THIRTY

SAVAGE'S HANGOVER was just beginning to fade when he pulled up at the edge of the proposed data center site. After Monroe's mysterious letter and her request to look into the land acquisition, he'd figured he'd better give Caldwell a call.

They'd arranged to meet out here. Caldwell's suggestion, and to be honest, Savage had relished the excuse to get some fresh air.

A black SUV was parked a little farther down. A well-built, expensively suited African American man who he assumed was Andre Caldwell stood beside it, talking on his phone. They'd never met in person, but given the press the data center had received, he'd seen a couple of photos.

Savage killed the engine and stepped out of the Suburban. He surveyed the land stretching out in front of him. Acres of open ground scattered with scrub and knee-high grass, the wind moving through it in slow ripples. Prime land. He supposed it was only a matter of time before somebody snatched it up.

Caldwell ended his call as Savage approached, slipping the device into his jacket pocket and extending a hand. The man looked taller and more impressive in the flesh.

"Sheriff. It's good to meet you in person. Appreciate you coming out." His grip was firm, confident.

Savage nodded. "You said you had something to show me?"

Caldwell gestured out across the land. "Let's take a walk."

They began to stroll, the grassy ground uneven underfoot. Caldwell seemed very much at ease, and Savage got the impression he knew this property extremely well. He'd probably walked every inch of it during Larry Quince's company's survey.

"I know there's a lot of controversy around this project," Caldwell began. "A lot of assumptions. So, I wanted you to see it for yourself. This isn't some industrial monstrosity we're planning."

Savage glanced at him. "Nobody's seen the plans yet. That's half the problem. People are fearful of what they don't know."

If they had, they might be even more concerned.

Caldwell gave a faint smile. "People hear 'data center' and picture smokestacks and concrete blocks. That's not what we're building." He made a sweeping gesture with his hand. "Low-profile structures. Environmentally controlled. Minimal footprint compared to traditional industry."

Savage said nothing.

"There'll be extensive landscaping with tree cover and water recycling systems. Times have changed, Sheriff. Technology has changed, even in this industry. Infrastructure is not like it once was."

Savage kept walking, scanning the land around them. He loved the wide, open spaces in southern Colorado, so different from Denver where he'd lived for most of his life. Out here, he felt like he could breathe.

Savage stopped and turned to Caldwell. "How much do you know about the history of this property?"

The other man seemed surprised by the question.

"Not a lot. The company I represent have put an offer in on the land. The planning committee will approve the sale if the vote goes in our favor."

"Well, I know something about it." Savage put his hands on his hips. "This land used to belong to the Garrity family. They were ranchers and long-time residents of Hawk's Landing."

Caldwell simply watched him and waited for him to finish.

"Twenty years ago, a different company wanted to develop this land, but the owners wouldn't sell. Coincidently, a short time later there was a fire. A bad one. The whole family died and the ranch house burned to the ground."

"That's terrible." Caldwell frowned and shook his head. "But what's that got to do with me, or my company?"

"I'm telling you so you understand the emotion behind this proposal. People out here have long memories. There were rumors that the Garrity fire wasn't an accident."

"What happened to the interest in their land?" Caldwell asked.

"Nothing, clearly." Savage gestured to the fields around them. "For some reason the sale fell through. Blocked by certain members on the council, or local pressure groups. Who knows? But there was no development out here."

"Until now," Caldwell said.

Savage met his gaze. "Exactly."

Caldwell let out a measured breath. "I get it. This is pristine land. Beautiful country. People don't want to see a data center here."

"You must be used to resistance," Savage surmised. He'd underestimated the man. Caldwell was sensitive to the issues, but he was a businessman first and foremost. He'd do what he needed to get this proposal passed.

If Savage was worried beforehand, he was even more so now.

"We were expecting this," he admitted with a rueful grin. "Even with Commissioner Albright brokering the deal."

Savage stopped. "Albright is on board with this?'

"Yeah. He's the one who approached us with the idea. We were looking for the space in which to launch this project, and out of all the options, this one was the most promising."

Now that was interesting.

Savage recalled his conversation with Albright at the community center. He had mentioned jobs, he'd mentioned progress. That one couldn't fight it forever. Was that because he was backing it?

Savage had to admit he was surprised. Albright was a member of the Guardians. Part of the old guard that Nancy Monroe so despised. Which meant the Guardians weren't aligned on this. Savage massaged his forehead. How would that play out?

They resumed walking.

"You've seen the changes, Sheriff," Caldwell went on. "You've seen what's happening to your town, to a lot of small towns like this one. Farms are failing. Businesses are closing. People are leaving because there's nothing here for them."

Savage flinched—he didn't need reminding.

"The drought hit hard," Caldwell continued. "Harder than most people realize. A lot of people haven't recovered. Some won't."

Savage kicked at a patch of dry soil. It broke apart too easily.

"And your data center fixes that?" He glanced across at Caldwell.

"Not fix, but it will help," Caldwell predicted. "It'll provide construction jobs to start with, followed by permanent positions—maintenance, security, technical roles. Not to mention the secondary impact. Housing, services, supply chains. It will bring prosperity back into the area."

Savage looked out across the land again, trying to picture it.

Buildings. Infrastructure. Power lines.

Change.

"Not everyone wants that," he said at last.

"No," Caldwell agreed. "They don't. And I get why. Change is uncomfortable. It means having to get used to something new. Something different. But what's the alternative? If you don't do anything..." He shook his head. "That's how towns die."

Savage said nothing.

"Think about the younger generation," Caldwell continued in his rich baritone voice. He would have made a good motivational speaker. "The kids growing up here... what's keeping them around? What future do they have?"

Savage thought of Connor. What kind of place would Hawk's Landing be when he was older? A dead-end ghost town? Or a thriving tech hub? Was there anything in between?

"You're assuming your proposal gets approved," he argued.

Caldwell's face broke into a wide grin. "I'm optimistic."

Savage gave a soft snort. "You'll have a fight on your hands. There are many influential people opposed to this."

"A small contingent, from what I've heard," Caldwell remarked dryly. "But you can't halt progress. You need us, Sheriff. The town needs us if it wants to not just survive but thrive."

That remained to be seen. Caldwell talked a good game, though.

A gust moved across the land, stirring the dry grass.

Savage's gaze drifted past him, out toward the far edge of the property. In the distance, half-obscured by a cluster of scrub and a lone, wind-bent tree, stood what was left of the old ranch house.

It was little more than a blackened shell now. The roof had long since collapsed, and the walls, or what remained of them, stood warped and skeletal against the horizon. No one had rebuilt it, but it hadn't been torn down either. It just sat there, rotting in plain sight. A monstrosity no one wanted to touch.

Savage was aware that kids came out here sometimes. Dared each other to go inside. There were rumors the place was haunted, that people had heard wailing. But it was probably just the wind. Still, with enough time, it became folklore.

"Okay, Caldwell." Savage dragged his attention back to the topic at hand. "You've made your point. What do you want from me?"

"Less opposition would be nice." The man from D.C. chuckled. "I'm just asking that you're open to the possibility, that's all."

Savage frowned. "I didn't say I wasn't."

"No, you didn't say anything 'cause you wouldn't take my calls," he countered, shooting Savage a knowing look.

He guessed the guy had a point.

Savage gestured to where the Suburban was parked. "Look, this has been... enlightening, but I've got to head back."

Caldwell nodded. "Sure. I'll walk with you."

They strode back through the tall grass, the weak fall sun on their backs.

"I hope I can count on your vote, Sheriff," Caldwell said, once they got to their vehicles.

"Good to meet you, Caldwell." Savage shook his hand, not committing either way. One thing he did know was the developer wasn't at all what he'd expected.

"And you, Sheriff."

Caldwell raised a hand as Savage climbed into the Suburban and then stood there watching as he drove away.

THE HIGHWAY WAS quiet as Savage headed back toward town. Mid-afternoon, most people still at work. Kids still in school.

Savage leaned his head back, one hand resting loosely on the wheel, his mind turning over everything Caldwell had said. About Albright backing the deal. The community divided. The town caught somewhere between survival and change.

It felt bigger than a simple development proposal now, as he was sure had been Caldwell's intention.

It was because he was so lost in thought that he didn't immediately notice the black SUV creeping up behind him. It was only when it appeared in the rearview mirror that he glanced up and frowned.

What the hell?

It was coming in quick, closing the distance in seconds. Damn fool driver.

He eased off the gas, giving it room to pass.

It didn't. Instead, it edged ever closer until the bumpers were almost touching.

Savage tightened his grip on the wheel and swore under his breath. He couldn't see the driver on account of the low sun behind him. It looked like the driver was wearing a cap pulled low to hide his face.

Savage veered to the right, tires crunching the edge of the shoulder, offering more space in which to pass, but the SUV stayed right where it was.

What the hell was this guy playing at?

Savage gritted his teeth. He thought about Zales and the hit-and-run. The truck running the red light and not stopping. His pulse raced as he focused on the road.

The SUV surged forward. The impact was expected, but still a shock. A brutal jolt that slammed into the rear of the Suburban and sent a shockwave through the chassis. Savage lurched forward against the seatbelt as the vehicle fishtailed beneath him, the tires screeching as he fought to keep control.

Another hit followed, harder this time, snapping the rear end sideways. The Suburban swerved toward the shoulder, gravel spitting out from beneath the tires as the road fell away at the edge.

He wrenched the wheel, trying to correct, but there was no traction out here, no grip, just loose dirt and stones giving way beneath him.

The third impact drove into him like a battering ram.

The world tilted violently as the Suburban flew off the road, the front end dipping as it struck the uneven ground beyond the shoulder. For a split second, everything hung weightless and suspended before momentum took over.

The vehicle rolled. Metal screamed as it scraped against the asphalt, glass shattering inward in a spray of fragments. The sky and ground traded places in a blur of motion, the horizon spinning wildly as Savage was thrown against the restraints.

Over and over it went until, finally, the Suburban crashed down into the ditch with a crushing impact, landing upside down in a cloud of dust and debris.

THIRTY-ONE

LUCAS'S PHONE buzzed on his desk.

"It's the sheriff," he said, as he reached for it.

"I was wondering where he'd got to." Sinclair glanced at the fading light outside the window. "He should have been back ages ago."

"Hey, Sheriff," Lucas answered.

"I'm going to need you and Thorpe to come out here."

"Sure. Where are you?"

"Not sure exactly. On the interstate, somewhere past the ten-mile marker."

"You broken down?"

"You could say that. Some bastard drove me off the road."

Lucas jumped out of his chair. "What? Are you hurt?"

Both Sinclair and Thorpe swung around.

"I'm fine. Suburban's not. How soon can you get out here?"

"Leaving now," he said, nodding to Thorpe, who shut his laptop with a snap.

"What?" Sinclair demanded, also on her feet.

"Sheriff was forced off the road. He's fine," he said quickly, seeing their faces. "But he needs us out there."

"What about me?" Sinclair asked.

Lucas shook his head.

Sinclair slumped back into her seat. "I suppose somebody's got to hold the fort."

Lucas grabbed his keys, pulled on his jacket, and headed for the door. Thorpe, holding a field bag he'd grabbed from beneath his desk, was right behind him.

THEY LOCATED the wreck in a shallow ditch about thirty yards from the road, its dark hull facing upwards like an overturned wounded animal.

Lucas veered over onto the shoulder, kicking up gravel as he came to a hard stop.

"Jesus," Thorpe muttered, gazing across him at the scene of the accident. This was more than just being driven off the road. He could see by the twisted wreckage that the Suburban had ploughed into the ditch and cartwheeled out of it. Several times, by the looks of things.

Both men jumped out. The damage was worse up close.

The windshield had caved inward, spiderwebbed glass blown out across the ground. The engine ticked faintly, undercarriage exposed. The roof had taken the brunt of the impact, crushed in along one side. Dirt and dry grass clung to the bodywork, smeared across the panels from where it had rolled.

A trail of gouged earth marked its path off the road.

Savage sat a few yards away, propped against a low rock, one leg stretched out in front of him, the other bent. His shirt was streaked with dust, one sleeve torn. Blood had dried along his temple, a darker line trailing down the side of his face. His right hand was worse. Cut up, raw, flecked with dirt and glass. But he was upright and conscious.

Lucas let out a long breath as they walked over. "You okay, Sheriff?"

Savage gave a short nod. "I've been better."

Thorpe gestured to the Suburban. "What the hell happened?"

Savage shifted against the rock but didn't try to stand up. "I was on my way back from meeting Caldwell when this black SUV came up behind me. Fast. I pulled over, but it didn't try to pass."

Thorpe's jaw tightened. "What then?"

"Rammed into me. Three times. Forced me off the road."

Thorpe backtracked to the edge of the asphalt and crouched down, studying the surface. "I don't see any brake marks," he called. "He wasn't trying to stop."

Savage shook his head. "Nope."

Lucas was beginning to see why Savage had asked for Thorpe. The guy clearly knew about this kind of thing. He got the impression this wasn't the first time they'd been in this situation.

Thorpe moved a little farther along, tracing the disturbed gravel where the Suburban had left the road. He knelt, running his fingers lightly over the surface, then stood and walked toward the wreck.

Lucas followed his gaze.

"Could it have been Caldwell?" he asked.

Savage shook his head, then grimaced. "Nah. He was still on site when I left. Anyway, it wasn't his vehicle. This one was wider, boxier."

Thorpe nodded, circling the overturned vehicle. He stopped at the rear panel and leaned in closer.

"There," he said.

Lucas went over and crouched down beside him. "What you got?"

Then he saw it. A smear of black paint streaked along the crumpled metal. It wasn't from the Suburban.

"Some black paint," Thorpe said. "Must have transferred on impact."

Savage pushed himself a little more upright. “Enough for a sample?”

Thorpe nodded. “Might get a make or model if we’re lucky, but black SUVs aren’t exactly rare.”

Lucas straightened. “You get a look at the driver?”

“Nah. Sun was in my eyes, and he was wearing a cap. I couldn’t make out his face.”

Lucas gave a faint nod.

“There are some tire tracks here,” Thorpe said, scanning the road. Looks like a four-wheel drive.”

“Can you identify the treads?” Lucas asked.

“Standard tread,” he said, brushing dust from his hands. “Nothing distinctive from what I can see. Could belong to half the county.”

Lucas swore under his breath.

He held a hand down to Savage. “Let’s get you to the hospital.”

Savage accepted his hand, and Lucas hauled him to his feet. “I’m fine. I’ll clean up back at the office.”

“You sure? You’re cut up and bleeding.”

Savage dusted himself off. “This was a warning. Means we’re getting close.”

Lucas glanced at Thorpe, who just shrugged. Neither of them could tell the sheriff what to do.

“Okay, I’ll call a tow company and get the Suburban picked up,” Thorpe pulled out his phone.

Savage nodded. “Thanks. Let’s go. We’ve got work to do.”

“I WANT you to dig deeper into that fire twenty years ago,” Savage said as they drove back to town. Lucas, who was behind the wheel, glanced across at him.

Lucas frowned. “Something happen with Caldwell?”

“Not really, but I saw the ranch house. It was a charred shell. Never been out there before.”

Lucas nodded. He'd seen it with his aunt Clara when they'd ridden out on horseback the day he'd gone to speak to her about it.

"Talk to O'Riley. I want him to go out there and take a look."

"I looked up the old fire chief," Lucas told him. After everything that had happened, he'd shelved what Hogarth had told him. "He said the fire was an accident and that his verdict stands. He was pretty emphatic about it."

Savage grunted. "I want a second opinion."

"Sure, I'll give O'Riley a call when we get back."

He'd met the Fire Chief several times during the wildfires earlier in the year and socially, with Sinclair. He was a great guy. Easygoing, smart, and very capable.

"You think we'll find proof of arson after all this time?" Thorpe asked from the backseat.

Savage shrugged. "Who knows? Ask Pearl Turner to meet you out there. She's got some forensic fire experience, and I'd like her opinion too."

Lucas nodded, eyes on the road. Maybe his aunt had been right all along.

"Say we find evidence of arson, what then?" Lucas asked, as they turned off to Hawk's Landing. "Does it affect this vote?"

Savage shrugged. "Maybe. Nancy Monroe wanted us to look into it properly, so that's what we're doing. I think if there's any suggestion that the land was acquired illegally, she won't touch it."

"She's pretty by-the-book, isn't she?" Lucas asked.

Savage nodded. "It's refreshing after Beckett."

Lucas knew Nancy Monroe wanted to distance the local government from the corruption of her predecessor. Consequently, she had zero tolerance for small-town politics and off-the-books agreements. Everything had to be transparent and accountable.

"What does that mean for the data center?" Lucas asked, as he turned onto Main Street.

"I don't know. I guess that depends on what we find," Savage said.

THIRTY-TWO

"ALBRIGHT BROKERED THE DEAL?" Barb spluttered, once the initial fuss over his appearance was over and he'd cleaned up. "I find that hard to believe."

"It's true. Caldwell told me himself," Savage said, attempting to tuck in a stray piece of bandage. He'd spent the last twenty minutes at the sink, working shards of glass out of his palm with a pair of tweezers. Then he'd rinsed the cuts under cold running water until the worst of the dirt and blood was gone. He'd found the department's antiseptic, poured more of it on than necessary, and wrapped his hand. It wasn't the most professional of jobs, but it would hold.

Barb had been worried about tetanus, but he'd had a shot a few months back. The gash on his forehead wasn't as bad as it looked, although it did bring back his headache from that morning.

"But he's always been anti-development," she muttered, taking Savage's arm and rewrapping the last bit, tying it off properly.

"Didn't he oppose the earlier development on the Garrity land?" Sinclair asked.

"He did," Lucas said. "I looked into it. After the fire that killed the family, the property went up for auction. Albright leaned heavily on the council to purchase it. They outbid the development company that had been hoping to get it on the cheap."

"No doubt with the Guardians behind him," Barb said, letting Savage's arm go.

He gave a derisive snort. "The Guardians aren't as influential as they used to be. Besides, I think they're divided over this data center proposal."

"Really?" Barb arched a brow. "They spent years blocking the development on that land, and now he's pushing it through?"

"They must be if Albright is in favor of it," Savage pointed out.

Barb smoothed a jittery hand over her hair. "This just keeps getting worse. First Monroe asks you to look into the land deal, then Caldwell tries to sell you on it, and now someone runs you off the road." She shot him a concerned look. "When does it end?"

"Once the vote is passed," he predicted, not unkindly. "Or vetoed. Either way, it'll end with that."

She shook her head and sighed, then went back to her office.

"Do you think this was the same guy who took out Gregory?" Lucas nodded at Savage's bandaged hand.

"Or Zales," Thorpe said.

Savage gave a grim nod.

"But why come after you now?" Sinclair asked. "We've been investigating for over a week, ever since the Wilsons were shot. Why would he, they, whoever, try to run you off the road now?"

Savage thought for a moment. "Well, let's see. I'd just been to check out the land for the proposed data center."

Sinclair's voice was croaky. "You think this has got something to do with that?"

"Maybe." He scowled as the thought took hold. "Maybe it doesn't have anything to do with Gregory or the Wilsons. Could be someone is trying to stop me from investigating the fire."

Lucas drew in a breath. "That was twenty years ago."

"Yeah. But if that proves to be deliberate, the proposed vote could fall through. Nancy Monroe would take serious issue with allowing development on land acquired as a result of the murder of the previous owners."

Sinclair let out a breath. "Well, crap. I didn't think of that."

None of them had.

"Then we better get on that," Lucas said, swiveling back to his desk and reaching for his phone. "Before whoever is behind this goes in there and destroy what little evidence is left."

"If there is any after all this time," Thorpe muttered.

IT WAS after ten when they called it quits. Savage sent his team home, then took a couple more painkillers and sat in his office to see what he could find about former senior CIA officer Benjamin Vance.

There wasn't much. A few archived articles. A retirement notice buried in a *Washington Post* column. A photograph from years ago of Vance standing behind a podium, all sharp lines and controlled expression. The kind of man who didn't give much away.

Then nothing. No recent sightings. No interviews. No traceable footprint.

Savage leaned back in his chair, frowning. Men like that didn't just disappear unless they wanted to.

He started with the obvious. The wife.

It took him twenty minutes to find out her maiden name and another ten to track down a possible family connection in Arizona. He made the call, identifying himself, keeping it simple.

There was a pause on the other end when he mentioned Vance.

"You said Ben?" an older man asked, voice cautious.

"Yes, sir. Benjamin Vance."

Another pause. Longer this time.

"My sister passed in 2018," the man said eventually. "Cancer."

Savage let out a breath. "I'm sorry to hear that."

"Yeah." The man cleared his throat. "Haven't heard from Ben since the funeral. Not properly, anyway. He sent a card that first Christmas. After that... nothing."

"No forwarding address or contact details?"

"No. That was kind of his way." A dry note crept into the man's voice. "Wasn't a man you could easily get to know. Know what I mean?"

Savage did. "He have any habits? Places he liked? Anything that might point me in the right direction?" It was a longshot, but what the hell? This man was one of the few who'd actually known Vance.

Another pause.

"He liked to fish."

Savage sat up straight at his desk. "Fish, you say?"

"Bass. He was big into it. Used to disappear for days chasing tournaments, even before he retired. Mexico, Texas, anywhere there was water and no people." A faint chuckle. "I remember once, he said it was the only place he could think straight."

That was something.

"Do you know where in Mexico?" Savage asked.

"Not exactly. But I remember him talking about Lake El Salto. Said it was the best bass fishing in the world. Went down there more than once."

Savage wrote it down.

They spoke a little longer, but there wasn't much else. No numbers. No friends. No recent contact. When he hung up, Savage turned back to his computer and looked up Lake El Salto.

He pulled up what he could. Lodges, guides, fishing tours. Places that catered to Americans with money and time. Vance would have stood out. Not flashy, but regular. The kind of man who came back year after year.

Savage started making calls.

The first lodge had nothing. The second didn't answer. The third time he got through to an older guy who thankfully spoke pretty good English. He hesitated when Savage mentioned the name.

"Vance?" the man said. "Yeah, that rings a bell."

Savage sucked in a breath. "You know him?"

"I remember him. Tall guy, but quiet. Kept to himself. He came down a few seasons back. Didn't say much, but damn, he could fish." A pause. "Haven't seen him in a while, though."

"Did he leave a contact number?"

Another pause. Papers shuffling on the other end.

"Most of these guys do. Waiver forms, bookings..." The man trailed off, then came back. "Yeah. Got something here. Not sure if it's still good."

Savage felt his pulse kick up a notch.

"I'll take it."

The man read it out.

Savage wrote it down, then read it back to him, just to be sure.

When the call ended, he sat back, staring at the number on the page. Vance clearly hadn't wanted to be found. Was that because he knew something about Department Nine? Something that could get him killed?

Was that why he'd disappeared?

Savage picked up his cell phone. It was time to find out.

THIRTY-THREE

SAVAGE TYPED the number into his phone and hit the call button. It connected straight away. At least that was something. He'd half expected the number to be deactivated.

It rang several times, but nobody picked up.

Savage leaned back in his chair, groaning at the ache in his side. When he'd last checked, his ribs on the right were turning an interesting purple color. The pills were keeping the pain at bay, and while his head ached, he didn't have a concussion or anything. He'd gotten away with minimal injuries, thank God.

His gaze drifted through his open office door and to the crime board at the far end of the squad room. He didn't need to see it clearly to know what was on it.

The Wilsons. Gregory. Department Nine.

Come on...

Eight names.

Eight soldiers, five accounted for. The rest... who knew? As Lucas said, they could be anyone.

The line clicked and went to voicemail.

Shit.

He sat forward and prepared to leave a message.

"Benjamin Vance," he said after the tone. "This is Sheriff Dalton Savage, Hawk's Landing, Colorado. I'm working a double homicide, and I believe it may be connected to something you were involved with years ago."

He paused, choosing his next words carefully.

"I wouldn't be calling if it wasn't important. I need five minutes of your time. That's all. Call me back."

He ended the call. Hopefully that would be enough to entice Vance to call him back. If not, he'd just have to track him down another way.

THE AUTOMATIC PORCH light clicked on as he stepped up to his front door, keys in hand. He'd driven one of the department vehicles home since the Suburban was unlikely to see the road again. If it came back as a write-off, he'd have to get Barb to put in for a replacement.

Damn, his body ached. Ribs, hand, head. The beers from the night before still sat heavy behind his eyes. It had been a hell of a day.

Savage let himself in and went straight to the sink where he downed a full glass of water, kicked off his boots, and stumbled into the living room.

The house was cold, but he didn't bother to light a fire. He didn't have the energy to make anything to eat either. Instead, he took off his jacket, loosened his shirt and collapsed on the couch, pulling the throw on top of him. He'd lie here and rest for a minute, then he'd go to bed.

Closing his eyes, he replayed the events of the day in his head. Nancy Monroe... meeting Caldwell... the charred ranch house... the car wreck... Vance. His thoughts began to blur at the edges.

A shrill ringtone dragged him from his slumber.

He blinked, confused.

What the hell?

Then he remembered, he'd purposely switched his phone off silent in case the office emergency number diverted to his cell or Vance called back.

Reaching across the coffee table, he picked it up and squinted at the screen. Didn't recognize the number.

"Savage." His voice was rough.

A pause, and then an older, measured voice on the other end said, "You called me."

He pushed himself upright, the sleep falling away in an instant. "Vance?"

"Depends who's asking."

"Sheriff Savage from La Plata County. I left the message on your cell."

Silence stretched for a beat.

"Okay," Vance said finally. "You've got my attention. Make it quick."

Savage tried to compose his thoughts. "I've got a double homicide. Both victims were killed the same way. Two shots—one under the jaw, the other to the head. Classic double tap."

Nothing from the other end.

"There were no casings found at the scene. No signs of a struggle."

Still nothing.

"The shooter used nine mil, bonded rounds. My ME tells me it's a professional job." He let that sit for a while.

"Why are you asking me about it?"

"Don't you recognize the MO? After all, you've seen it before. Several times, in fact. In Istanbul, northern Iraq, and Cyprus."

The line was quiet for so long Savage wondered if the call had dropped.

"What do you want?" Vance asked, eventually. Savage could tell his tone had shifted. It was cautious now. Careful.

"Information."

"I can't give you that," he hissed.

"Why?"

"It has nothing to do with me," Vance said, more urgently now. "I left that world behind a long time ago."

Savage shook his head. "You may have left, but someone from that unit is still active, and they're killing residents in my county. I need to find out why."

"That's your problem, Sheriff."

"I think you can help me," Savage pressed. "You don't want these guys out there any more than I do. They're dangerous, but then you already know that."

No response.

Savage took a breath, then said, "Does the name Victor Gregory ring a bell?"

Silence.

"He's the third victim, although that's not in my jurisdiction. Someone took him out using the same MO. We've got a rogue assassin on the loose, Vance. Help me find them, and we can end this, once and for all."

When Vance finally spoke, his voice was like granite. "I can't help you."

Savage clenched his jaw. "Yes, you can. What you mean is you won't help me."

"I said I can't." A beat. "Leave it alone, Sheriff. That's my advice."

The line went dead.

Cursing under his breath, Savage lowered the phone. The lamp burned softly in the corner while it had started raining again outside. He sat in silence for a long time, listening to the pitter-patter against the windows.

He must have drifted off again because he was awakened by his phone a second time. This time it was the loud beep of a text message.

Groaning, he rolled onto his good side and reached for it. The message was from the same number.

Breath catching, he tapped on it, and an image loaded onto the screen. It was a photograph, taken a long time ago.

Of eight men.

Four at the back. Four in front. They were dressed in military fatigues and stood shoulder to shoulder. Their ages ranged from mid-twenties to mid-thirties, and they all had that hard-eyed stare that soldiers got when they'd seen too much.

His pulse quickened as he sat up, wide awake now.

Department Nine. It had to be.

He stared at the faces, scanning each one, looking for the man he already knew would be there. And the one he didn't.

THIRTY-FOUR

LUCAS PULLED up beside the old ranch house and killed the engine. He sat there for a moment, taking in the scale of disruption. From a distance, when he'd been on horseback, the place had looked like a ruin, but up close, it was far worse.

What had once been a family home was now little more than a skeletal frame. Blackened beams reached toward the pale sky like broken ribs. The roof had long since collapsed, leaving the structure open to the elements. Sunlight filtered through the gaps, casting uneven shadows across the ground, where weeds and scrub had forced their way through what remained of the floor.

Mason O'Riley stood a short distance away, hands resting on his hips. He studied the dilapidated structure, casting his professional eye over it. Assessing what remained.

Next to him, crouching near the edge of the foundation, was the forensic expert, Pearl Turner. She had a small kitbag open beside her, attention focused on the ground. They both looked around as he closed the door of his truck and made his way over.

Pearl got to her feet. "Hello, Deputy."

Mason shook his hand. "Lucas."

"Thanks for coming out," he said.

Mason gave a brief nod. "Sure. I've never been out here before. Heard about it, obviously. The old-timers tell stories about the bad ones. But this is my first time seeing it."

Pearl gestured to the wreckage. "What exactly are we looking for, Deputy?"

Lucas told them about the original incident report. "The detective in charge ruled it an accidental fire. The verdict was based on the fire chief's report that said the gas stove had been left on. Sheriff wants to know if that still holds up."

Mason nodded. "The former chief being Max Hogarth?"

"That's the one. I tried to ask him about it, but he shut me down. Said his report stands."

"It won't be easy to verify," Mason said with a skeptical smile. "It's been twenty years. There won't be much in the way of chemical evidence. Anything like gasoline would've burned off or evaporated a long time ago."

Pearl nodded in agreement. "I'll take samples, but Mason's right. We'll be lucky if we find anything like accelerant."

"I figured," Lucas said, glancing at Mason. "But there must be other ways to tell if it was deliberate or not."

Mason gave a nod. "You're right, and there are. If something doesn't add up, I'll let you know."

Pearl picked up the kitbag and stepped over a charred beam into what remained of the structure. "Let's get started," she said.

Mason followed her in, proceeding with caution. He inspected the structure as he went, laying his hand on the blackened remains of a wall.

Lucas came in behind them, picking his way through the debris, making sure to avoid anything loose or crumbling. The elements had added their own destructive force, and over time had worn down the structure even more.

Mason gestured to a section where the floor dipped and

remnants of piping protruded from the ground. "That would have been the kitchen."

Pearl crouched beside a section of exposed floor joist, running her gloved fingers along the surface. The wood there was deeply charred, blackened almost to the point of collapse.

"That's interesting," she murmured, frowning.

Lucas glanced down. "What is?"

She tapped the beam lightly with her knuckle. "You see how deep the charring goes? And how low it is?"

He nodded. "Yeah?"

"That suggests sustained, intense heat at floor level."

Mason moved toward what might have once been the side wall and examined it. "She's right. If this had been a gas build-up from the stove, you'd expect the fire to rise. Gas disperses upward. You'd get more damage higher up, not concentrated down there like that."

Pearl got up, stepped over a collapsed section of wall into what had once been a hallway, and dropped back down to the ground. "It's the same here."

Mason followed, crouching to take a closer look. "It's not what you would expect from a gas fire."

Lucas clenched his jaw. "Why not?"

Mason gestured to the walls. Despite the years of exposure, a faint pattern was still visible in the charred wood. Dark lines rose upward in a narrow V-shape. "Classic upward burn pattern. Look at the direction. It doesn't align with a single source. You've got multiple V-patterns across the structure, each pointing back to different origin points."

Pearl straightened. "This blaze didn't start in one place. I can't tell you how it started, but I can tell you it wasn't from the gas stove. Your fire chief was wrong."

She glanced at Mason, who gave a reluctant nod.

"Even if the stove was left on, the gas would've followed the path of least resistance," Mason added. "It would've spread through the open space. You wouldn't get isolated burn pockets like this, not without something deliberately directing it."

"There's no evidence of a pressure event," Pearl added, glancing around. "No blast pattern, no outward structural displacement—just sustained burning."

Lucas let out a slow breath. "So, the original report..."

"Doesn't hold up," Mason finished.

THIRTY-FIVE

"YOU'RE SURE?" Savage asked when Lucas told him what he'd discovered.

"Mason and Pearl were both a hundred percent," his deputy confirmed. "The fire was set deliberately. No doubt about it."

"I'm going to need a report," Savage said, running a hand over his jaw. "Something I can put in front of Monroe." At least he'd remembered to shave that morning, which helped him appear more respectable. Because the bruising didn't. The swelling around his eye had darkened overnight, while the cut above it had formed a scab, giving him the look of someone who'd taken a few rounds and come off second-best.

The purple bruising around his torso was so bad, he'd stopped looking at it.

After the text message from Vance, he'd managed to grab a few extra hours of shut-eye, then showered, dressed—both tentatively—and driven into work.

"You'll have them by this afternoon," Lucas told him. "They did say we should look at the autopsy report for soot in the airways and carbon monoxide levels in the blood. That tells you whether they were alive when the fire started… or if they were already dead."

"You get on that," Savage said, and turned back to the crime board where he'd stuck up a large print version of the photograph he'd received last night, which thankfully had been pretty good quality. "I didn't see an autopsy report in the file, but there must be one somewhere."

"What's this?" Lucas gestured to the board.

"Benjamin Vance came through," he replied. "This is a photograph of Department Nine."

"All eight men," Sinclair said, getting up from her desk to join them at the board. Beside it was the list of names Zales had given them.

"I'm matching them to the names." She pointed to the red lines she'd drawn connecting the name to the soldier on the image. "So far we have identified Victor Gregory, and the three men with criminal records. That leaves four unaccounted for."

"Then our killer is one of those." Lucas stared at the faces, searching for familiar features. Savage recognized the look. He'd done the same thing when he'd first seen it. "I don't recognize Ed Burges."

"He'd be younger then," Thorpe called across from where he was sitting. "I'm working on finding a younger photograph of Burges to compare it to."

Savage left them to get on with it and went back to his office and placed a call to Councilwoman Monroe. He got her assistant. Ms. Monroe was tied up in meetings all morning.

Savage didn't envy her. Politics was one side of this job he didn't enjoy and wasn't good at. He made an appointment with her for that afternoon and then got back to work.

"Dalton, I just heard from the auto repair shop." Barb stuck her head around the door. "I'm sorry to have to tell you this, but the Suburban is a write-off."

He sighed. Dammit. He'd had that vehicle ever since he'd been in

Hawk's Landing. They had history, and now it would end up on some scrapheap somewhere.

"Okay, thanks Barb." He couldn't help a pang of nostalgia. Seemed like everything came to an end eventually.

"Want me to put in a new purchase order? You need transportation."

He gave her a nod. "Yeah, you'd better."

SAVAGE WAS ABOUT to leave for his appointment with Councilwoman Monroe when Lucas knocked on his office door. He could tell by his deputy's expression that it was serious. "I've got something for you, Sheriff."

He beckoned him in. "This about the autopsy?"

"Yeah." He didn't sit down but instead thrust his hands into his pockets. "I had a hard time tracking down the medical examiner who performed it. Dr. Toby Bryant. Thorpe helped me in the end. Bryant's been off the grid for years. Turns out he moved to London shortly after the fire."

"London? Any particular reason?"

"Said he had family there, although we couldn't find anyone related to him living in Britain when we checked. Anyway, Thorpe traced him through some private consult that he signed off on soon after he arrived. It was the only slip-up, else we'd never have found him."

Savage frowned. "Okay."

"At first he didn't want to talk about it, but I explained that nobody knew I was contacting him, and it wouldn't go on any record anywhere."

"You think he was scared?" Savage asked. After what had happened to Zales, the guy had a right to be.

"Felt like it to me," Lucas said with a nod.

"What did he say?"

Lucas's jaw tensed. "Said it was hard to forget the Garrity case.

He'd never seen anything so terrible. The whole family, burned to death like that."

Savage nodded. It couldn't have been easy. "What about the smoke inhalation?"

"That's what I wanted to tell you." Lucas shifted. "Turns out they didn't die of smoke inhalation. None of them. They were shot."

"Shot?" Savage rubbed his temples. "They were all shot?"

He knew the answer before Lucas even said it.

"Submandibular and temple. Double tap. All four of 'em."

"Shit."

There was a long pause as he processed this. Eventually, Lucas said, "It's related, isn't it? Whoever murdered the Garrity family is operational again, here in Hawk's Landing."

Savage drew in a breath through his nostrils.

"It sure looks like it."

THIRTY-SIX

SAVAGE WALKED into the town hall exactly two minutes before his appointment. The corridor was quiet, the fluorescent lights casting a flat glow over bulletin boards cluttered with town notices, lost dog flyers, and photos from long-forgotten events. It felt more like a community space than an office.

Monroe's office was halfway down the hall.

He knocked, then let himself in after he heard her abrupt, "Come in."

She closed the folder she was reading and nodded at him. "Sheriff, I believe you have some news for me?" He liked that she got straight to the point.

Taking a seat opposite her, he opened his own folder and pulled out the one-page report O'Riley had written up outlining his findings. Pearl had sent her own, but since it said the same thing, he didn't bother handing that over as well.

"I have, and you're not going to like it."

Her gaze sharpened, and she sat back in her chair. "Okay. I'm listening."

"We looked into the fire at the Garrity family ranch, the previous owners of the land for the proposed data center."

"And?"

"The fire was started deliberately," he said, and slid O'Riley's report over the smooth, mahogany desk toward her.

She snatched it up, her nails clicking on the wood. He waited while she scanned it, her mouth flattening into a thin line.

"Arson?" She said, glancing up. "They're sure?"

"There is no doubt. It's all there in the report."

He hesitated, wondering if he ought to tell her about the victims, about the lack of smoke in their lungs, no carbon dioxide in their blood. The gunshot wounds. That they were dead long before the fire got to them.

He didn't want to lie, or withhold information, but this wasn't a criminal case and she wasn't the law. He was perfectly within his rights not to divulge information he didn't think relevant.

Edgar Zales's blood was on his hands. He didn't want to add Dr. Bryant's to it as well. Somehow, the people or organization behind Department Nine knew where to look. Thorpe had covered his tracks, and the fewer people who even knew about Dr. Bryant's existence, the better.

So, he kept quiet and waited for her reaction.

"This is bad," she whispered, more to herself than to him. "Very bad." It was the most self-doubting he'd ever seen in her. Usually so confident, it unsettled him, and he took pity.

"Listen, the family died and a distant relative inherited the land. He decided he didn't want the hassle, and it was auctioned off to the council for back taxes. We looked at the records. They bought it fair and square. There is no mismanagement of funds, no land grab, nothing to prevent the vote from going ahead."

He couldn't believe he was actually saying that, but it was true. Legally, there was no reason not to go ahead.

Ethically, that was another issue.

She looked up and blinked, as if only just realizing he was still there. "But they were murdered. I read the original incident report.

The fire broke out at night. Whoever committed arson must have known the family was there. That makes it murder."

He dipped his head. "Not going to disagree with you there."

"Crap."

He almost liked her at this moment, defenses down, hand in her hair. Human.

"Now what am I supposed to do? Those against the development are going to suck this up, milk it for all its worth and throw it back in our faces. Those pro-progress are going to ignore it and say that it doesn't make any difference. If the land was purchased fair and square, the vote should go ahead, like you said."

"That's why they pay you the big bucks," he deadpanned, even though it wasn't funny. He didn't envy the position she was in.

She sighed, seemingly lost in thought for a moment, then sat up and worked to pull herself together.

"That it?" She glanced across at him.

He nodded.

"Okay, then. Thanks for doing this for me. I almost wish I hadn't asked now."

"Better to know up front what you're in for," he said with a wry grin.

"You're right, because these things have a way of getting out whether you want them to or not."

He got to his feet. "Good luck, Councilwoman."

She didn't smile. "Thank you, Sheriff."

THE BREAKTHROUGH CAME when he got back to the office. Thorpe had stuck an earlier photograph of Ed Burges up on the board, alongside the picture of the eight men. Both Sinclair and Lucas studied it through a magnifying glass. Barb stood behind them, shaking her head. "I don't think it's him."

"You got something?" Savage asked.

"That guy is definitely familiar," Lucas insisted, shaking his head. "But I don't know why."

"I don't recognize him," Sinclair countered, then pointed at the photo of Burges. "And it sure doesn't look like him when he was young."

"I have to agree with Sinclair," Barb said, sighing at Savage. "What do you think?"

He studied the photograph of Burges, then the eight men. He could see what Lucas meant. The guy in the bottom row, second left did look familiar, but it wasn't Burges.

"Now that you mention it," he muttered, frowning.

Lucas nodded. "I'm glad it's not just me."

"Maybe he's just got one of those really common faces?" Sinclair suggested. "You know, there are people like that. You think you know them, but you don't."

Thorpe just shook his head and went back to work.

"What?" she threw up her hands when nobody answered.

"Okay, listen up," Savage said. "We need to talk about what Lucas found."

"The Garrity family?" Sinclair asked.

He nodded and perched against the far side of her desk. "I just lied to Councilwoman Monroe."

"Dalton!" chided Barb.

He raised a hand. "Okay, not lied so much as omitted to tell her the truth. I confirmed it was arson, but not that the family had been executed beforehand." He glanced around at the team. "That information cannot leave this room."

They stared at him.

"It's too dangerous," he continued. "We already know that whoever is responsible for the hit on the Wilsons—or whoever the target was—is keeping tabs on this department. Victor Gregory is already dead, and we don't want to add anyone else to that list. Edgar Zales gave us information, just like Gregory. We have to be careful who we contact, and who we tell about any of this."

"Not to mention Dr. Toby Bryant," Lucas said.

He nodded. "I don't want anything in the system about the doctor, the method of the victims' deaths, or what we're working on now."

"That Department Nine was responsible for the Garrity murders," Sinclair whispered.

"It was a government hit squad," Lucas said, rubbing his forehead. "That in itself is terrifying."

"I can't see why they'd want to take out an entire ranching family," Barb was wringing her hands.

"Unless they wanted the land," Sinclair pointed out.

"It's still outright murder." Lucas shook his head. "What unit would agree to that?"

"You're right, it doesn't make sense." Savage frowned.

"Unless it wasn't the whole unit," Thorpe said from his desk.

They all turned to stare at him.

"Think about it." He frowned. "One or two of the soldiers could have gone rogue, acted out on their own. Now the whole unit is in the firing line."

"That would make more sense," Savage admitted with a nod.

"Whoever it was must have had a reason," Lucas insisted.

"Maybe they had a couple of hundred thousand of them," Savage reasoned.

"You mean a paid job?" Lucas gazed at him, considering.

"He, or they, could have needed the money. Not many jobs for ex-soldiers out there."

Lucas gave a slow nod.

Sinclair stood up. "So, someone decided they wanted that land. They paid a hitman to take out the family and burn the place to the ground."

"Except nothing was ever done with the land," Barb said.

"Nothing was done because the town council outbid the development company," Savage reminded them.

"So, we're saying the development company paid to have the

Garrity family killed?" Sinclair ran a hand through her hair. "None of this makes any sense."

"I think it's starting to," Savage said after a beat.

They all swung their attention back to him.

"I mean, we don't know who yet, but it could be the Wilsons knew who was responsible for the family's assassination. Maybe they'd seen or heard something, and that's why they were targeted."

"We're back to the Wilsons now?" Barb asked, shaking her head.

"Okay, maybe not them, but whoever the real target was," Savage amended. "Either way, that could be why the assassin was in town. He had to stop them from talking."

"Why would they say anything now?" Lucas spread his hands. "It's been twenty years."

"Because of the proposed data center," Savage said.

Thorpe was nodding slowly. "So that if someone like Nancy Monroe looked into it, the secret would stay buried. They wouldn't be able to tell their account of what happened."

"Except now we know," Lucas finished. "Too bad for them."

"Yeah. Ironically, we probably wouldn't have looked into it in so much detail if it hadn't been for that letter Nancy received—or the fact I was forced off the road."

"Or the noise Clara McBride was making," Barb added, then glanced at Lucas. "No offense."

He shrugged. "None taken."

"The letter," Sinclair whispered. "What if the real target wrote the letter? Maybe that was what the killer was trying to prevent." She glanced from Savage to the others.

He snapped his fingers and pointed. "You could be on the right track there. I need to get another look at that letter."

"So, not the Wilsons?" Barb said, heading back to her office. "Since they were dead already."

"Not the Wilsons, no," Savage corrected, shooting her an apologetic grin.

"Then the person who wrote the letter is the one we should be looking for," Lucas said, getting up. "He's the one who knew what happened twenty years ago. He's the one they tried to silence."

"But they screwed it up," Thorpe added. "And he—whoever he is—realized there was a hit out on him, tracked Gregory to the casino, and shot him first."

They all stared at each other.

"I think we're getting there," Savage murmured. "Finally."

THIRTY-SEVEN

THEY ALL STAYED LATE, extrapolating on their theory. All except Barb, who had left to go to a friend's seventieth birthday celebration.

The sun had long since set, and the street outside was shadowed in darkness. The fairy lights from the Halloween festivities had been taken down, and with the rain over the last few days, Main Street was dotted with puddles and trapped water that resembled oil slicks. It didn't look very inviting anyway.

Savage had to admit, every which way they analyzed it, their latest theory did make a horrible kind of sense.

"Let's assume it was one or two guys and not the entire unit," Lucas said, as they all sat staring at the crime board. "Someone still had to have hired them. If it wasn't the government, then who?"

"A private client," Savage guessed. "It had to be. Someone connected to the development company."

"Okay, sure," Sinclair said. "I get that this proposed data center might tie back to the fire, but won't whoever ordered the original hit be long-gone? It's not even the same company, is it?"

"That's what we need to find out." Savage glanced at Thorpe.

"Already ahead of you." Thorpe shot them a smug look, but then his expression faded. "It's not the same company. Unfortunately, that firm dissolved about eighteen months after the fire."

"Someone wanted to cover their tracks," Savage murmured.

"Who owned it?" Lucas asked.

Thorpe hesitated. "That's where it gets tricky. What's online is patchy. Just summary filings, not a full director list."

Sinclair frowned. "Nothing?"

"Not digitally," Thorpe said. "Most of the detailed records from back then were never scanned. You'd have to pull the original filings from county or state archives."

"So, we don't know who was running it," Savage said.

"I've got a lead," Thorpe replied. "The name 'West' shows up tied to the registration. Gareth West, likely the primary contact. After that, it goes thin. Could be family-run, could be fronts. No way to confirm without the original documents."

Sinclair raised an eyebrow. "Think they hired those mercenaries to start the fire?"

Thorpe gave a small shrug. "If they were in financial trouble—and it looks like they were—that land deal might've been their last shot. But right now, it's just a theory."

Savage exhaled. "We need something solid."

"I'll have to go digging for it," Thorpe said. "County clerk's office, maybe the assessor's records. If the full filings weren't digitized, they'll be sitting in a box somewhere."

Savage nodded. "That's a good idea." It would do Thorpe good to get away from the office for a while. Unfortunately, anything like that would be closed by now. "Head over first thing in the morning."

Thorpe gave a mock salute.

He saw Sinclair massaging her arm, while stifling a yawn. He could barely keep his own eyes open.

"Okay, let's call it for today. We're all beat. We can pick this up tomorrow."

It was Lucas's turn on call, but since they didn't have anyone in custody, they could all go home for the night.

SAVAGE GOT HOME to find three missed calls from Becca on the answering machine, and one message. He wasn't ready to talk yet. Doubtful if he ever would be.

Where did you go from there? She was seeing someone else, and it was over between them. It was clear now that she'd never meant to get back together. When she'd left, it had been final for her.

He'd been the one clinging onto the hope that they'd be able to reconcile. Be a family again.

His stalked past the machine to the refrigerator and took out a can of beer. Opening it, he took a long pull and lowered his bruised and weary body onto one of the chairs around the kitchen table. He needed a long, hot shower, then he'd have to redress the wound on his hand.

It wasn't settling as fast as he'd hoped. Maybe there were some shards of glass left in there. If it didn't start healing soon, he'd have to get Ray to take a look at it. As far as he was concerned, the medical examiner was better than a hospital.

It had been six months since Becca had left. Didn't seem like long enough for her to meet someone new.

Then again, Becca was an expert at starting over.

He frowned at the direction his thoughts had taken. He didn't like thinking badly of her, but wasn't that exactly what she'd done in Philly? Packed up and disappeared. Left a psycho-therapy practice, a home, a life... to come out to Colorado to start again under a different name.

She'd left her past behind, until it had caught up to her.

Unfortunately, she hadn't trusted him enough to tell him. To let him help her.

Now she'd done the same thing again, except this time she'd taken Connor with her. He didn't know who she was dating, or even if it was serious, but he did know he didn't want anybody else raising his son.

Hating the bad taste in his mouth, he downed the rest of the can, then crunched it and hurled it at the trash can. It bounced off the side and rattled across the floor. He stared at it for a moment, then went to the bathroom to take a shower.

THIRTY-EIGHT

THE CALL to the department phone got diverted to Lucas' cell. He rubbed his eyes and sat up. It was still dark outside. Glancing at his phone on the nightstand, he saw that it was five thirty-six in the morning.

Reaching for it, he answered. "Hello, this is Deputy McBride."

"Deputy, it's Jonas Half Moon. From Ridgewater Casino."

Lucas swung his legs over the side of the bed, already more awake. "Hey, Jonas. What's going on?"

Five-thirty was an unusual time for an emergency, and the casino was on the res. Not their jurisdiction.

There was a brief pause on the other end, then Jonas said, "Sam Walking Deer asked me to call you. Housekeeping found something under one of the beds on the fifth floor that he thought you should see."

"Was it one of the rooms occupied the night of the shooting?" He couldn't think of any other reason why the casino manager would suggest calling them.

"Uh-huh."

Lucas reached for the lamp and flicked it on. "What kind of something?"

"I think you ought to get down here and see for yourself."

A bullet? A gun? A piece of clothing? A long list of possible items connected to the shooting ran through his mind.

"Okay, I'm on my way."

HALF AN HOUR LATER, Lucas pulled his pickup into the casino parking lot. The asphalt glistened from the overnight rain. He opened his door and stepped out into a puddle.

Great.

He shook off his pant leg, then strode to the front entrance. Even at this hour, the casino was alive with sound, lights and chatter. It felt like he was stepping into another world, an alternative universe where the fun never stopped.

Maybe not fun, he corrected, as he headed past the chaos of one-armed bandits to the escalators. But something.

Jonas waited for him on the mezzanine floor, just in front of the reception desk. He nodded as Lucas approached.

"I got here as quick as I could."

"Follow me."

Jonas led him to the security suite where they'd watched the footage the night of the shooting. "Housekeeping found it in room 523. The one the old guy stayed in."

"I remember," Lucas said. "The one who ordered room service and had a hearing aid."

Jonas gave a curt nod.

Lucas frowned, wondering what they could have found under his bed. A sock, maybe? A box of medication?

Once inside, Jonas gestured to the desk where a brown paper bag lay. It looked like a normal shopping bag. "What's inside?" he asked.

"Take a look."

Lucas stepped forward and peered into the bag. Inside lay a soft, furry thing that resembled a dead hamster.

He glanced up at Jonas. "What is it?"

Jonas fixed him with a hard stare. "It's a wig."

LUCAS CALLED Savage on his way to the sheriff's department. Ahead of him, the sky was just turning a pale peach as dawn debated making an appearance. Beside him on the passenger seat was the brown paper bag.

It rang a few times before Savage answered. "Yeah?"

"Sheriff, it's Lucas."

"What's up?" He sounded groggy.

Lucas told him what had happened. Savage wasted no time.

"I'll meet you at the office."

"HOW'D they know it's from the guy in room 523?" Savage asked. It was a good question, and one Lucas had asked of Jonas.

"That room's only had one other guest in it since the shooting," he told his boss. "A woman on her way to visit friends in Durango, and she had a full head of hair. No need for a man's hairpiece."

"Fair enough," Savage muttered as he stared inside the bag. Lucas had opted not to move it at all, in case he compromised what DNA might be on there.

"It looks like the hair the old guy had," he said, gesturing. "Don't you think?"

"I'm trying to recall the footage."

Lucas pulled out a still and laid it on Savage's desk. "I got Jonas to print off a copy. It's not the clearest, but it's the best we could get."

"Good thinking." Savage picked it up and stared at it for a long time. Lucas noticed he used his left hand, since the right was still bandaged. "You're right. It's identical."

Lucas put his hands on his hips. "Which begs the question: Was the old guy wearing it because he was bald, or was he wearing it because he was in disguise?"

Savage stared at him. "Normally I'd say it was likely the former but given that a man was shot and killed in that hotel the very same night, I'm going for disguise."

Lucas nodded. "That's what I thought too."

"Jonas did well to call us," Savage remarked, walking around and easing himself into his chair behind the desk. He grimaced as he did so.

Lucas frowned. Savage still hadn't gone to the hospital to get checked out after the accident, and he'd always suspected he'd played down the extent of his injuries.

"It was Sam Walking Deer who told him to give us a shout. He thought it was strange and didn't want to call the Feds."

Savage snorted. "Who was staying in room 523?"

"The booking was under Thomas Harrow," Lucas told him. "The address was a retirement facility in Bayfield."

"You check it out?"

"I was just about to when you arrived."

"Okay, we need to check if that's legit first, before we jump to any assumptions."

Lucas headed for the door. "On it."

He left the sheriff alone in his office, staring at the still of the old man, and logged on to his computer. Five minutes later, he had the information he needed.

"The Happy Valley Retirement Home has no record of a Thomas Harrow living there," Lucas called.

Savage came out of his office just as the door opened and Thorpe hurried in.

"I got your message," he said, nodding to Lucas. "Thanks for calling me."

At Savage's surprised look, Lucas explained. "I know you wanted him to go to Denver, but I thought we might need his expertise."

"Good thinking," Savage murmured.

"It's unlikely Thomas Harrow is his real name," Lucas said to Thorpe, who took the still and hurried over to his desk. Within seconds, he'd logged on, and his fingers were flying over the keyboard.

"I'll see if I can find a Thomas Harrow in La Plata County," he said, speaking slowly as he typed.

Savage walked over to the crime board. "Hard to imagine the guy without hair, and twenty years younger."

"I know, I tried that too," Lucas said, joining him.

"Nothing on the State Voter Registration Database or the DMV," Thorpe said, glancing up. "I'll try the county assessor next and the criminal database."

"I can do that," Lucas said, taking a seat at his desk.

Savage didn't move from the board.

A short while later, Thorpe swiveled around. "Doesn't look like any property is registered in the name of Thomas Harrow."

"He's clean. No record," Lucas said.

Thorpe glanced over at Savage. "Looks like our old guy is a ghost."

"That tracks," Lucas said, after a long beat. "If he was part of the hit squad, he'd know how to live off the grid."

Thorpe stood up. "You want me to dive deeper on this guy, or head to Denver? I can make it in three and a half, four hours if I get going now."

"Isn't there someone at Denver PD who can look for the records for us?" Lucas suggested.

Savage narrowed his gaze. "Not the PD, but I do know a guy there who could do it. Remember Grayson Carter?"

"Who's he?" Lucas asked.

"A lawyer who went undercover in the Crimson Angels," Thorpe said.

Savage nodded.

Lucas snorted. "Now that's a story I need to hear."

"Will tell you when this is over." Thorpe shot him a grin and turned back to his computer. "I'm just glad I'm spared the trip to Denver."

"I've got to get hold of him first," Savage said, and disappeared into his office.

The door opened and Sinclair came in. She stared at them, surprised to find them all in so early.

"What did I miss?"

Lucas filled her in, while Thorpe glanced up every now and then to add some extra details.

"Holy smokes," she said, slumping onto her chair. "So, he was pretending this whole time, and he was the shooter?"

"Looks like it," Lucas said grimly. "We should have checked him out more thoroughly. I was fooled by the walking stick and the damn hearing aid."

"We all were," Thorpe said.

Lucas shook his head. "I know, but I went back to take another look. It was my job to vet all the guests, and I missed it."

"How were you supposed to know it was the hunched-up old guy?" Sinclair asked. "Especially since there were other suspects."

That was true. They'd been distracted by several other guests who did have skeletons in their closets. Ironically, the one that hadn't was the shooter. That should have been a bright red warning sign in itself.

Sinclair wandered over to Thorpe's desk to look at his screen. "You can't find any record of him?"

He didn't look up. "Not yet."

She picked up the still of the old guy from the footage and studied it. "Why d'you have a picture of him?"

Lucas frowned at her. "Who?"

"The guy from Maple Ridge Street. You know, Buddy's neighbor."

Lucas stared at her as the penny dropped. Thorpe stopped typing and looked up. They both stared at the photograph and then yelled, "Sheriff!"

THIRTY-NINE

"WHAT?" Savage asked, rushing out of his office.

"Sinclair knows who the shooter is," Lucas told him, pointing to Sinclair.

"You do?"

"This is the shooter?" She frowned, then held her hand up to cover his hair. "Yeah, I'm sure it's him."

"The guy who lives next to Ed Burges," Lucas said. "Remember, the one who was in the yard when we drove up?"

Savage remembered him. The potted plant. Nice guy.

He peered in. "Really?"

"Shit," Lucas exclaimed, turning toward the board. "That's why I recognized him. Bottom row, second to the right? A younger version, but he's the guy who told us where number forty-six was."

Savage grabbed the photograph from Sinclair and went over to the board. Once there, he held it up.

"It's definitely him," she said, standing beside him. "Look, he even has that little mole there, just under his right eye."

Savage looked closer. She was right. There was a mole. It

appeared on the still and the photograph of the younger version of Thomas Harrow.

The eyes were the same too. A telltale sign. Same shape, less wrinkled, of course. Even though the color was impossible to make out on either image.

Thorpe looked at them. “Do we know what number Maple Ridge Street he lived at?”

“There were no numbers anywhere,” Sinclair reminded him.

“It was two doors down and there were no houses on the opposite side of the street,” Lucas said. “So, I’m guessing forty-four or forty-eight.”

Thorpe got to work. Less than a minute later, he slammed his hand down on his desk, making them jump.

“I have a Harold Thomas,” he said, spinning around so fast his glasses slid down his nose. “And guess what? He lives at number *forty-six* Maple Ridge Street.”

“Holy shit!” Sinclair’s hand flew to her mouth.

Harold Thomas. Thomas Harrow.

It was close enough.

“He lied to us,” Savage hissed. “He knew exactly who we were. That’s why he directed us to Ed Burges’s place, hoping we wouldn’t realize it wasn’t number forty-six.”

“And we didn’t,” Sinclair said with a groan. “Because none of them had freaking numbers on them.”

Lucas bit his lip. “I bet he removed the second half of that number himself.”

Savage turned back to check the board. “Son of a—! Harold Thomas is one of the names on Zales’s list.” A double confirmation if they ever needed one.

Sinclair turned to look, then gulped.

“Now what?” she whispered, her face ashen.

Savage stuck the grainy still on the whiteboard, then stared into the killer’s eyes.

“Now, we go get the bastard.”

. . .

THEY TOOK TWO VEHICLES. Savage in the borrowed cruiser, Lucas driving his truck with Sinclair riding shotgun.

They sped across town in close convoy, and Savage was five minutes out when Thorpe's voice came over the in-car radio. "Harold Thomas changed his name in 2012, a couple of years after the unit disbanded. Now that I know his real name, I've got some background info on the suspect."

"Shoot," Savage said, hands gripping the wheel.

"The years he spent in the unit are redacted, as you can imagine," Thorpe said, "but he started out in infantry, then moved into special ops. He was thirty-five when he was recruited for Department Nine. One of the oldest in the unit."

"That would make him fifty-one now," Savage said, frowning. Hardly the old man they'd seen in the casino footage. Amazing what a limp and a wig could do.

He clenched his jaw. Harold Thomas had taken them all for fools.

"Sheriff, there's something else," Thorpe added. "Not sure how it happened, but he had a leg blown off in Iraq. Was medically discharged."

"That explains the limp," Savage gritted. "The guy must have a prosthetic."

"The cane was real," Thorpe said.

"Must be."

"So, this guy, Harold Thomas, was the original target?" Thorpe hadn't been with them on their first visit to Ed Burges's house. "Doesn't look like he'd be much of a threat. Especially not with one leg."

Savage gave a loud grunt. "Someone obviously thought different."

"I guess not all damage is done with guns," Thorpe mused. "It was what he knew that made him dangerous."

Savage didn't reply. The guy in the yard had seemed personable.

It had only been a few minutes, but he didn't strike Savage as a cold-blooded murderer.

"He must have been one of the men who set fire to the ranch house all those years ago."

"Hard to believe, looking at him now," Thorpe said.

"Believe it," Savage gritted out as he took the final corner onto Maple Ridge Street. "He managed to fool all of us."

He accelerated down the street, then braked hard outside Harold Thomas's house, tires spitting gravel as the vehicle skidded to a stop.

"Spread out," Savage barked as they piled out, weapons drawn.

Lucas moved left without hesitation, cutting around the side of the property, while Sinclair peeled off the other way, her hand steady on her sidearm as she scanned the yard.

Savage took the front. The place felt wrong. It was too quiet. No movement, no voices, just the low hum of the freeway in the distance.

Weapon up, he moved along the short path to the door, boots crunching lightly on the gravel.

He knocked once, hard. "Sheriff's department!"

Nothing.

He tried again, louder this time. "Harold Thomas! Open the door!"

Still nothing.

Savage stepped back and tried to look through the windows, but the curtains were drawn. Chances were the guy had bolted. If he'd known who they were the first time, no way had he stuck around for them to figure it out and come back.

He went back to the door and tried the handle, but it was locked.

"Fuck this," he muttered, and drove his shoulder into the door. The impact shuddered through his injured ribs, making him wince.

Gritting his teeth, he tried again. This time, the frame gave way with a sharp crack. The lock splintered as the door flew inward.

He stepped through, weapon raised. "Sheriff's department! Come out with your hands up, Thomas!"

Silence met him.

He moved through the house methodically, clearing each room as he went. Pausing at doorways, slicing the corners before stepping through, eyes tracking left to right. Bedroom. Bathroom. Hall closet.

Nothing.

When he was satisfied, he lowered his weapon and crossed into the kitchen, unlocking the back door.

Lucas slipped inside without a word and moved past him, picking up the sweep. His deputy checked it again, room by room. Slower this time, more deliberate.

Savage stayed where he was, listening, but the house was silent. Just the light footsteps of Lucas moving through the rooms.

Outside, Sinclair would be in position, covering both exits in case the suspect was hiding and decided to make a run for it.

"It's clear," Lucas confirmed a moment later, stepping back into the room.

Savage gave a short nod and holstered his sidearm.

"Bring Sinclair in."

Lucas headed for the front door.

Savage took a long look around the living room. It was neat. Not just tidy but ordered. Everything had its place. The surfaces were clean and uncluttered. Chairs pushed in exactly where they should be. A blanket over the couch to protect it, or to cover the stains.

"There are no dishes in the sink either," Lucas commented. "The place is spotless. Definitely a military man."

Savage motioned to a wheelchair positioned inside the living room door. "The guy clearly had mobility issues."

"Still managed to take out Gregory though. And fool us," Lucas said, unable to keep the admiration out of his voice.

Savage scowled. Did he share Lucas's sentiment? He wasn't sure.

"He's a killer and an arsonist," he reminded his deputy, who gave a subdued nod.

"Yeah, sorry."

But he'd also been targeted, then had taken out his would-be assassin. Not an easy feat, especially with his disability. Not even in the ten years Savage had worked homicide at Denver PD had a perpetrator so thoroughly pulled the wool over his eyes.

He left the living room and went into the bedroom, checking the closet. Looked like most of Thomas's stuff was still there.

"He probably had a go-bag under his bed, and when he sent us to Buddy's that day, he got the hell out of here," Lucas said, coming in behind him.

"Could be."

Savage moved to the desk positioned under the window. It was a simple, functional piece with two drawers and nothing left out on the surface.

He pulled the left one open.

Inside, everything was laid out with care. A small stack of photographs, the edges worn from frequent handling. A couple of service medals. A notebook.

Savage flicked through the photographs first. He found several of Thomas and his army buddies, arms around each other's shoulders, squinting into the sun. Vacation shots, somewhere tropical. A couple of a pretty brunette with a warm smile. He wondered what had happened to her.

"Look at this." He showed Lucas a similar photograph to the one Vance had sent him. The eight men of Department Nine. This one was more relaxed. A few of the men were even smiling. Thomas was wearing a different colored cap to the rest of them.

"He must have been the team leader," Lucas said, peering over his shoulder at the picture. "That's why he's older."

Savage took out the medals and laid them out on top of the desk. Thomas had chosen not to display them. There was no sentimentality here. They were just objects, kept and forgotten.

Next, he pulled out the notebook and flicked through it. It wasn't a diary. There were no personal entries, just pages of printed handwriting. He frowned, recognizing it.

"It was Harold Thomas who sent that letter to Nancy Monroe," he said, staring at the lopsided script.

"It was?" Sinclair came into the room.

"He must have wanted her to look into the fire," Lucas murmured.

Savage frowned. "Seems so."

"But why would he have done that, if he was involved in it?" Sinclair asked.

Savage just shook his head. He didn't have the answers.

At the back of the drawer, he found a burner phone. It was an old model with the battery removed.

"Doesn't look used," he said, studying it. The thing hadn't been operational in years, judging by the state of it. He put it back and moved over to the right-hand drawer.

That one contained a stack of clippings. Looked to be from newspapers, magazines, and random publications. Picking them up, he thumbed through them.

"Take a look at this," he murmured, handing the top one to Sinclair, who was closest.

"It's the ranch fire," she whispered, staring at the article dated twenty years back.

"There are other write-ups here," Savage said, spreading them out on the surface of the desk.

Some of them were old and faded. The aftermath of the Garrity fire. Articles in the local paper about the tragedy. A piece on the family, all four smiling at the camera.

"He kept everything," Sinclair murmured, looking through them.

"Look at this." She handed him what appeared to be the corporate filings of a company called Pioneer Holdings LLC.

As Savage scanned it, a chill crept down his spine. "This is the development company Thorpe was looking into." The one he was going to ask Grayson Carter to look into in Denver. There was no need now. It was all here.

"The partners' names are listed there," Lucas said, pointing to the top of the sheet.

"Gareth West, that's who Thorpe mentioned," he murmured, and then his gaze fell on the name below, and he froze.

"Clifford Albright," Lucas murmured, glancing at Savage.

"As in Commissioner Albright?" Sinclair asked.

Savage stared at the name. "This can't be right. Albright was the one who persuaded the town council to bid on the property when it went up for auction."

"So why is he listed as a partner in that very same company?" Lucas asked, his voice low.

Savage shook his head. None of this made sense. He picked up another company report. This one newer, with a hard, shiny cover and Caldwell's company's logo on it. He paged through it, knowing what he'd find before he saw it.

Albright. This time he was on the board of Caldwell's Washington-based conglomerate. Plus, he'd been the one to broker the deal with the town council. Caldwell had told him that himself.

Savage felt his stomach churn. Seems Albright had been biding his time, waiting for another opportunity to get his hands on the Garrity family land.

Sinclair opened a drawer in the nightstand. "Look at this."

He turned around. She held up an empty box of bullets.

"Same type used in Gregory's murder," Lucas noted grimly.

Sinclair spread her arms around the room. "He didn't just start collecting this stuff recently. He's been holding onto all this for years."

"He wants justice," Savage said, nodding at the empty box.

"For the Wilsons?" she asked.

"For the Garritys."

"Huh?" Sinclair turned to look at him. "I thought he was involved in that?"

"He was," Lucas agreed. "He must have been. Why else would he have been targeted?"

"I'm not sure he was," Savage said, thinking out loud. "I think it was Harold Thomas's unit that set fire to that ranch house," he said as it suddenly became clear. All the pieces somehow slotted into place. "But Thomas couldn't live with it. It haunted him, what they'd done."

Lucas stared at the articles scattered over the desk. "That's why he kept all this stuff? Guilt?"

"He's been sitting on this secret for twenty years," Savage murmured. "That's why he was targeted."

"But why now?" Sinclair asked, coming over. "After all this time?"

"Because with the proposed data center, the original land grab might come under scrutiny, particularly by protesters. And Harold Thomas had ample evidence to back that up."

"Except Gregory shot the Wilsons instead," Sinclair whispered.

"Thomas recognized the MO straight away," Savage continued, thinking out loud. "He knew those bullets were meant for him."

"So he hunted down Gregory and took him out," Lucas finished.

Savage gave a tight nod.

"But he's not done." He nodded to the empty box of ammunition in Sinclair's hand. "I think he's gone to kill Commissioner Albright."

FORTY

"YOU THINK Commissioner Albright ordered the hit?" Lucas asked as Albright's estate came into view. The property sprawled across the lower slopes of the San Juan range, which bordered the town to the north. The electric gate was already opening by the time they reached it, security responding to Lucas's call.

"I'd bet good money on it," Savage replied, slowing down. "He probably instigated the plot to burn down the Garrity place too."

"I thought he was friends with the family," Sinclair said from where she sat in the back.

Savage's jaw tightened. "He was."

The gate itself was a heavy wrought-iron structure, reinforced with modern hydraulics. More ranch fortress than private residence. Discreet cameras tracked them, pivoting with quiet precision as they came closer.

Two bulky men in suits stood just inside, watching them drive up and come to a stop.

Savage lowered his window, and the security guard bent to peer inside the vehicle, scanning the occupants.

"Sheriff," he said with a nod. "We were informed you were coming. Is there a problem?"

"We need to see the Commissioner," Savage said.

The man hesitated. "He left a couple hours ago."

Savage bit back a curse. "You know where?"

"No, sorry. He doesn't tell us where he's going."

Some security detail, Savage thought.

A younger man appeared on the drive. He was in his mid-thirties, light brown hair, with a tanned face. He wheeled an expensive-looking mountain bike toward the gate. Savage recognized him as Albright's son, Clifford Junior.

"Hey, Sheriff," Clifford Jr. said, coming over. "Can I help you?"

"We're looking for your father," Savage said, opening the door and standing up. It was Clifford Jr. who'd lost his fiancé to the Frost Killer nearly a year ago now. "You know where he is?"

"Golf course," the young man replied, one hand resting on the handlebars. "He's playing with Andre Caldwell."

Even better, Savage thought sagely. "Which course?"

"San Juan Ridge," Clifford Jr. said, pointing west. "Ten minutes from here."

Savage was already getting back into the car.

THE GOLF COURSE spread out across a wide stretch of rolling land. Manicured greens stood out like an oasis in the dry terrain. Sprinklers ticked rhythmically in the distance, catching the light in fine arcs that shimmered like mist.

Savage pulled up outside the clubhouse, and Lucas and Sinclair had the doors open before the engine had fully cut. Savage got out and quickly scanned the lot, but he didn't know what car Harold Thomas drove.

Was he already here?

They hurried into the clubhouse, bursting through the double doors into the airconditioned lobby. The receptionist, who was on the telephone, looked up in surprise, along with several startled golfers. Conversations faltered mid-sentence.

"Sheriff's department." Savage flashed his badge as they strode over to the counter. "We need to find Commissioner Albright. Where is he?"

The woman ended the call and consulted a booking sheet on the desk in front of her. "He checked in about an hour ago. He's out on the course."

"Which hole?" Savage asked.

She glanced down again. "They began on the front nine... looks like he'd be around the sixth or seventh fairway by now."

Savage nodded. "We need a cart."

"Of course," she said quickly, reaching for a radio. "I'll have someone bring—"

"No time," Sinclair said, as two golfers pulled up outside the double glass doors that led out onto the green. She started to move. "Come on. We'll take those."

They commandeered the two carts from the surprised golfers and drove hard out onto the course. The small, rubber tires hummed over the trimmed grass as they cut across to the far side of the fairway.

Savage looked ahead, squinting into the low afternoon sun. Clusters of cottonwoods and aspens lined the fairways, their leaves trembling in the breeze. It was a lovely fall afternoon, perfect for a round of golf.

"See anything?" Lucas called from the second cart where he sat beside Sinclair. The electric motor whined as she pushed it to its limit.

"Nothing yet," Savage replied.

They crested a slight rise, and the land opened up ahead of them. A sand bunker sat just off to the right. Something in it caught Savage's eye.

"Hold up," he said, shielding his eyes to get a better look.

"Shit! Over there. Look."

A man lay in the center, his head protected by a baseball cap. It was hard to see who it was from this distance.

They veered toward the bunker and brought the carts to a stop. Savage hopped out first, moving quickly toward the man, weapon drawn.

Sinclair and Lucas followed right behind him.

"It's not Albright," he called, bending down to check for a pulse.

It was Caldwell.

The businessman lay on his stomach in the sand, one arm twisted awkwardly beneath him, the other stretched above his head. The light windbreaker he wore was dusted with fine grit, his neatly pressed polo and slacks coated in a thin layer of sand. A dark mark showed at his temple. He was unconscious.

Savage pressed two fingers to his neck, then nodded.

"He's alive."

Sinclair was already on her phone. "I'll call an ambulance."

Savage stood up and scanned the fairway, but Albright was nowhere to be seen.

FORTY-ONE

"STAY WITH HIM," Savage said, his voice tight. "Lucas, with me."

He didn't wait for a reply, just set off at a jog toward the line of trees bordering the green. It was the only real cover for a hundred yards in any direction. If Thomas had Albright, that's where they'd be.

Lucas followed without question, weapon ready.

The neat perfection of the golf course gave way to scrub, patches of fallen leaves, and exposed roots as they hit the rougher terrain at the edge of the fairway.

Savage slowed as they reached the first line of trees. Lucas fell back, slowing to a halt. They paused, listening, weapons drawn.

At first there was nothing, except the mild breeze rustling what foliage was left on the trees, but then he heard it. Voices. Faint, but unmistakable.

He beckoned Lucas forward, and they angled left, following the sounds to a copse of trees. They stepped lightly, careful to avoid dry twigs and loose stones.

Eventually, the two men came into view.

Savage looked at Lucas and gestured for him to move right, while he stayed where he was and waited until his deputy had snuck out of sight.

Albright stood with his back to them, arms raised in a defensive gesture.

Standing opposite, his gun aimed at Albright's head, was Harold Thomas.

He looked different up-close than he had that day in the yard. Leaner. Harder. There was a toughness to him that spoke of discipline and training, despite his age and the prosthetic leg. Or perhaps because of it.

No hint of the old man now. If it hadn't been for that wig, they might have never pieced it together.

Savage stepped into the edge of the clearing. "Game's up, Harrow. Or should I call you Harold Thomas?"

Harrow's gaze flicked over to his, but his grip on the gun didn't change. Neither did his aim. "Haven't used that name in a long time."

"Harrow, then."

"How'd you find me?"

"It was the wig. And my deputy recognized you from a photograph."

He gave a slow nod. "Darn wig. Realized I'd left it behind but it was too late by then. Knew my futile attempts wouldn't hold you back for long."

"Thank God you're here," Albright said. "For God's sake. Shoot him." Savage wondered where the commissioner's cane was. The stoop seemed to have disappeared too, and he stood more upright than he had last time he'd seen him outside the community building. Seemed Harrow wasn't the only one pretending.

Savage ignored him. "We found the articles in your house. We know you were there, when the fire was set."

"He lied to us," Harrow's gaze was hard as it fixed on Albright. "He told us the family wasn't home. That they'd gone away. The fire was supposed to be a warning, that's all. No one was supposed to die."

"Who lied? Albright?"

"For God's sake, man. Why are you indulging him?" Albright demanded.

"Of course, Albright. Who else?" spat Harrow, gesturing with his gun. His expression was haunted. "I tried to save them. I tried to get to them, but Victor had taken care of that."

"They were already dead?" Savage guessed.

"Shot twice. Even the kids." His eyes tightened as if he couldn't stand to think about it. But he wasn't so inexperienced as to close them. Not even for a second. "It wasn't even a government sanctioned op."

Savage frowned. "Then what? A personal favor?"

"Albright said it was one last op. A side mission. We only agreed because it was a privately paid job. The unit had already been decommissioned. We weren't even supposed to be there." His voice cracked, and he levelled his gun at Albright.

Savage turned to the commissioner. "You gave the order to murder the Garrity family."

"I don't know what he's talking about," Albright snapped, hands still in the air. "The man's clearly unhinged."

Harrow didn't look unhinged. Upset, angry, determined, yes. But not unhinged.

"I've seen the evidence," Savage told him. "You tried to bury it, but you were a partner in Pioneer Holdings. Your company wanted to develop that land. That's irrefutable."

"So what?" Albright snapped. "That's not a crime."

Savage kept his gun trained on Harrow.

"I haven't done anything wrong," Albright insisted. "This madman accosted me on the golf course and is holding me hostage. Arrest him!"

Savage didn't move.

Through the trees, he saw Lucas in position.

"I have a couple of questions of my own, first," Savage said.

Albright looked between Harrow and Savage. "What is this? A joke? Some conspiracy you've cooked up?"

"Nope. My questions are for you, and this seems like as good a time as any, since you're not going anywhere."

Harrow smirked.

"You're crazy," Albright fumed. "I'm going to have your badge for this, Savage."

"I don't think so." Savage studied him, seeing him for who he really was. A corrupt, murdering politician. No better than Beckett. Exactly the type of person Nancy Monroe hated and had vowed to remove from office.

"Why did you have the council outbid your own company?"

He scoffed. "Isn't it obvious? I was a Guardian of the town. Recently recruited into the most powerful organization in the county. I couldn't let it come out that I was a partner in the development company—even a silent one. It was just smart business sense."

"You chose membership to the Guardians over all that money?"

Savage wasn't buying it.

"I wasn't a commissioner at that point," Albright explained. "I worked for the Agency."

The pieces suddenly clicked into place. "Department Nine. That was your idea?"

Albright started, then muttered. "Damn Zales."

"It was your idea, wasn't it?" Savage said. "An elite squadron of soldiers who could go where normal units couldn't."

"You got it." Harrow nodded. "He was our liaison officer. We reported directly to him."

"And you were the team leader?" Savage asked.

Harrow gave a tight nod. "Yeah. We thought we were a force for good. That's what was sold to us anyway. We were serving our country, eliminating those that posed a real and present threat. Except it was all bullshit."

"Southern Iraq?" Savage asked.

Harrow eyed him. "You know about that?"

"Zales told me."

Albright's mouth flattened into a thin line. Savage didn't miss it. He swung to Albright. "That's why you had him murdered, isn't it?"

"Who's Zales?" Albright asked.

"That won't work, Albright. I spoke to Zales myself. I have the folder he kept. It contains everything. Missions, dates, locations, and outcomes. It's all there."

He shrugged. "It's not a secret I worked for the Agency."

"But after the failure of Department Nine, you wanted out. So, you started Pioneer Holdings with Gareth West."

"Again, that's not a secret. I had every right to start a company to develop land in my home county."

"Except you never got the chance."

"I got another opportunity," he corrected. "State Commissioner. I had to make a choice. That's all it was."

"That's far from all it was, Albright," Savage said. "What about Robert Carver? Heart failure in Tucson four years back. That you?"

Albright didn't answer.

"What about me? Did you try to run me off the road?"

The tightness around his mouth told Savage what he needed to know.

Christ. Edgar Zales, Robert Carver. How many people who knew about Department Nine had died of natural causes once Albright decided to clean house?

"Sheriff, where are you going with this?" He almost sounded bored. "Can't you just arrest this man and get this over with?"

"I'm afraid not, Commissioner. You see, you're both under arrest. You for the murder of the Garrity family and the suspected murder of Frank and Sarah Wilson and Edgar Zales." And Robert Carver, he added silently to himself, although he knew that would never be proven.

"He doesn't deserve to live," Harrow growled.

"And you're under arrest for the murder of Victor Gregory," Savage added.

Albright laughed and lowered his hands. "How are you going to arrest both of us, Sheriff?" He began to back away, a smirk on his face.

Harrow stiffened. "Don't move, Albright, or I'll shoot that smug look off your face."

"I think the Sheriff will shoot you first, my friend." He took another step backwards towards the golf course.

Savage nodded to Lucas, who stepped out from the tree line to the left of Harrow so he had a clear line of sight.

"Stay right there and keep your hands where I can see them," he ordered, training his gun on the Commissioner.

Albright froze.

"You really think I came alone?" Savage shook his head.

Harrow's finger tightened over the trigger.

"Don't," Savage snapped, clocking the miniscule movement. "Don't do it, Harrow. He's not worth it."

"I disagree with you there, Sheriff," Harrow said, his arm steady. His gaze didn't waver. Not this time. He was going to pull the goddamn trigger. Savage saw it in his stance, in the glint of determination in his eyes.

And he wasn't sure he could stop him.

FORTY-TWO

"YOU PULL THAT TRIGGER, and he wins." Savage took a step forward.

Harrow didn't move.

"You're giving him what he wants," Savage said. "By shooting him, you're the killer and he's the victim. Is that how you want this to end?"

"I want it to end with him in a body bag," Harrow said, gritting his teeth. "Like those civilians. That couple. Those kids."

"It won't change what happened," Savage pointed out softly.

"I know, but it'll make me feel a hell of a lot better."

"You sure about that?"

Harrow's grip tightened. "I'm willing to find out."

Albright's smirk faltered.

"You'll be saving him a trial," Savage said. "The truth won't come out. Instead, you'll go down as a murderer."

Savage knew he'd hit the right note when Harrow's arm lowered, just fractionally. He was thinking about it.

"Let me take him into custody. We do this the right way. Everyone will know he's a fraud."

"I am not a fraud," Albright shouted.

"They'll know what he did. To the Garrity family, to the Wilsons."

The arm lowered even more. Savage let out a breath he hadn't realized he'd been holding. "That's it. Easy."

Harrow sighed, and let the gun flip around his trigger finger, so it hung downwards. Then he held it out to Savage. "Okay. You win, Sheriff. I'm tired of the lines being blurred. We'll do this your way, but he'd better get what's coming to him, or I'm going to hunt him down and handle it myself."

"Noted," Savage said, moving in. Lucas did the same, stepping past Harrow toward Albright.

Savage confiscated Harrow's gun and shoved it down the back of his jeans, then he took Harrow by the arm.

"Hands behind your back," Lucas said, taking Albright's arm. He holstered his weapon and reached for his cuffs.

Savage caught the shift in Albright's eyes a split second too late. Not toward the gun. Lower. To Lucas's right leg.

The limp. Albright had clocked it.

The Commissioner pivoted hard, breaking Lucas's grip, and drove the heel of his shoe straight down onto the side of the deputy's right knee.

Lucas grunted as his leg buckled beneath him. He dropped to one knee, his hand snatching for the holster half a second behind.

Albright was already there. He tore the sidearm free and stepped behind the kneeling deputy in one fluid motion, the muzzle pressed hard against the side of Lucas's head.

"Drop your weapon, Sheriff," Albright said. His voice was different now. Lower. Steadier. The frail commissioner act was gone. The man underneath was someone Savage had never seen. "Or your deputy dies on this golf course."

"You wouldn't shoot him," Savage tried, not moving. "Not in cold blood."

"Try me," he said, flipping off the safety.

Lucas held still, his eyes on Savage. There was a question in his gaze.

Savage knew Lucas was more than capable of turning the tables on Albright, even with the bad leg under him, but what if the Commissioner pulled the trigger? The man was a ruthless killer. He'd ordered the hit on Harrow, on Zales, even hired his own unit to burn the Garrity ranch to the ground with everyone in it.

As much as he trusted his deputy, he couldn't take a chance.

Savage gave a minute shake of his head and threw his firearm to the ground.

"Now kick it away from you," Albright ordered.

Savage did so, his jaw tight.

Lucas didn't move. He just stood there, hands in the air, waiting for whatever came next.

"That's it. Now I'm going to head out of here, and none of you are going to try to stop me."

Albright stepped backwards, dragging Lucas with him. Lucas didn't resist. Savage admired his nerves, but then the Marine had seen plenty of action. He knew how to stay calm under pressure. Assess the situation. Adapt.

"You're letting him get away?" Harrow hissed, as Savage didn't make a move to stop them.

"For now," he murmured. He was pretty sure Sinclair would have left Caldwell with the paramedics and come after them. She probably had her weapon trained on Albright right now.

On cue, he heard a female voice shout, "Drop it, Albright. Put your gun on the ground now!"

Albright turned and fired in the direction of her voice. He was about to get off a second shot when Savage reached behind him for Harrow's gun.

He was too late. The ex-Department Nine soldier got there first. Savage was powerless to react as Harrow twisted around and let off two shots in rapid succession.

"No!" he shouted, as Albright's head exploded in a cloud of red mist.

Lucas, who'd grabbed him before he'd been shot, lowered the commissioner to the ground.

Behind them, Sinclair approached, shaken but standing.

"You okay?" Savage asked, glancing away from Albright's body, where a dark stain was already spreading out beneath him.

She gave a shaky nod. "Geez, that was close. One more shot, and he'd have got me." She turned to Harrow. "You saved my life."

"I did what I should have done a long time ago." Harrow handed Savage the gun, then held out both his hands. Savage took it, then snapped the cuffs on him.

"You might want to rephrase that in court," he muttered.

Lucas straightened up, wincing as he tried to put pressure on his injured leg.

"You all right?" Savage asked. Not only was he in pain, but he was covered in Albright's blood.

"Yeah." Lucas adjusted his stance, then ran his sleeve across his forehead, smearing it even more. "Sorry about that. He took me by surprise. I could have taken him down," he said, glancing at Harrow.

"Too risky," Savage said.

He'd made his decision and was sticking to it. Had Lucas failed, and Albright pulled the trigger, he'd be looking at a dead deputy right now, instead of a dead corrupt politician.

"Sorry about the mess," Harrow said, as Savage led him back toward the fairway.

FORTY-THREE

SAVAGE STOOD with a fresh cup of coffee in his hand, watching the steam curl up off the surface, and let himself enjoy the small victory. After the week he'd had, he'd take it.

It was just after nine in the morning, three days since the golf course. He'd slept badly each of those nights, and the bruises around his ribs had settled into a deep, ugly green that made every breath a reminder.

But the case was closed. Albright was in the morgue. Harrow was in federal custody, having been transferred up to Denver yesterday once the Bureau realized what they had on their hands. Two agents from the Denver field office had spent the better part of an afternoon in his office taking copies of everything in the Zales folder.

They'd looked very interested when he'd handed over the photograph from Vance.

He hoped they did something with it.

Out in the squad room, Sinclair was on the phone, her bandaged forearm propped on the desk. The bandage was smaller now, just a strip of gauze under her cuff. Lucas stood at the crime board, taking down the photographs one by one and stacking them in a folder for the prosecutor's office. Thorpe was at his computer, headphones on, doing whatever it was he did when he didn't want to be interrupted.

Barb was at the front desk, sorting through the morning's mail.

It almost felt normal.

"Sheriff?" Barb called through. "Councilwoman Monroe and the mayor are here to see you."

Savage straightened. He'd been expecting Monroe. Not McAllister.

"Send them in."

He moved back to his office and set the coffee down on the desk just as Barb showed them through. Monroe came in first, dressed in a dove-grey suit, her usual leather folio under one arm. McAllister followed, red in the face from the cold and looking like a man who hadn't slept much either.

Savage gestured to the two chairs opposite him. "Morning. Take a seat."

Monroe sat. McAllister stayed standing for a beat, then dropped heavily into the other chair, as if reluctantly conceding the point.

"Sheriff," Monroe said. "First, I want to thank you. What you and your team uncovered was ... considerable. I don't think any of us expected it."

"You're welcome," he said. "Though I doubt the gratitude is universal."

She gave a small, tight smile. "No. It isn't." There was a brief pause. "There's one thing I don't fully understand?"

Savage arched an eyebrow. "Yeah?"

"Why did Albright move on Harrow now, twenty years after the fact? Was it the data center proposal?"

He gave a tight nod. "That's exactly right. When the Washington crowd showed up wanting to build their data center on that same parcel of land, that's what kicked it off. Suddenly there were protesters. Reporters from Durango." He nodded to her. "You were asking the kind of questions he didn't want asked."

"And Harold Thomas?"

"Harold Thomas was the one man left who was actually inside that ranch when it was set alight. He lived two miles from the crime scene, holding a folder of newspaper clippings he'd kept for two decades."

She let out a long exhale and shook her head. "So he sent the letter to me?"

"Yeah. You replaced Beckett, and you were the first councilwoman in twenty years who didn't owe Albright anything. Harrow was looking for someone to take a fresh look at that fire, and you were his only pick."

McAllister shifted in his chair. "We're here about the vote, Sheriff."

Of course they were.

Savage sat down behind his desk. "Go on."

"It needs to go ahead," McAllister said. "As scheduled. We've already had two delays this fall, and the council can't keep kicking it down the road. The town's lost enough momentum on this as it is."

Savage looked at Monroe. "That your position too?"

She let out a slow breath. "It's not what I would choose, no. Personally, I'd like more time. The dust hasn't settled. Albright was a sitting state commissioner with ties to that land going back twenty years, and the public deserves to understand the full picture before we sign off on anything that builds on top of it."

"Then delay it," Savage said.

"I *can't*. The planning application has met all its statutory requirements. The land is in council ownership, free and clear. The acquisition twenty years ago was lawful, even if the circumstances behind it weren't. Legally, there's no basis to halt the vote."

"So, it goes ahead," Savage said flatly.

"It goes ahead," Monroe confirmed. "But it goes ahead with everything on the record. The fire, the original investigation, Albright's involvement, the company he founded with Gareth West, the lot. I want this council to vote with full knowledge of what it's voting on. If they still approve the development after that, then they do it with their eyes open and their constituents will judge them accordingly."

McAllister cleared his throat. "That's a lot of detail to put into the public record."

"It's a lot of detail that's going to come out anyway," Monroe said evenly. "You can have it come out now, in front of a council vote, or you can have it come out three months from now in the press while we're halfway through breaking ground. I prefer the former."

McAllister opened his mouth, then closed it again.

Savage almost smiled. He was beginning to like Nancy Monroe.

"When?" he asked.

"Two weeks Thursday," Monroe said. "Seven o'clock, council chambers. Open session. We'll take public comment for the first hour and the vote afterwards."

"You'll have a full house," Savage said.

"I'm counting on it."

There was a brief silence. McAllister fidgeted with his cufflink. Monroe sat very still, watching Savage.

"How's Mr. Caldwell?" she asked eventually.

"Alive. Bad concussion. Doctors are holding him at La Plata for observation, but they're telling me he'll be fine. Walked out of his room yesterday afternoon to argue with a nurse about the breakfast menu, so I'd say his personality survived intact."

Monroe gave a faint, dry laugh. "That sounds like him."

"He'll be released later this week. He's already asked when he can get back to work."

"And is he—" she paused, choosing her words. "Is he being looked at? In connection with any of this?"

Savage shook his head. "Far as I can tell, he's clean. Albright recruited his company because the land was already in council hands and he had the relationships to broker the deal. Caldwell didn't know the history. He was doing his job."

"Good," she said. "I'd like to see at least one person walk away from this without a stain."

McAllister stood up. "Well. We'll let you get on, Sheriff. I imagine you've got plenty to be doing."

"Some," Savage agreed.

Monroe rose more slowly. She paused at the door, then turned back.

"For what it's worth," she said, "I think the vote is going to fail. The council won't pass it once they hear the full story. Neither will the public."

Savage tilted his head. "You could be wrong."

"I could," she allowed. "But I don't think I am."

She gave him a small nod and followed McAllister out.

SAVAGE WAITED until he heard the front door close behind them, then picked up his coffee and walked back out into the squad room. Sinclair had finished her call. Lucas had stopped what he was doing and was leaning against his desk. Even Thorpe had taken off his headphones.

"Well?" Sinclair asked.

"Vote's on for two weeks Thursday. Monroe's going to put everything we found into the public record before they vote."

Lucas let out a low whistle. "Clara's going to lose her mind."

"Clara's going to be at that council meeting with bells on," Savage said. "And she won't be the only one."

Barb appeared from the front office with a small stack of cards in her hand. "Dalton, before I forget. The Wilsons' funeral is Friday. Eleven o'clock at Birch Hill. Quentin called this morning to confirm."

Savage nodded. "He coming back out for it?"

"He's already here. Flew in last night." Barb hesitated. "He wanted me to pass on his thanks. For telling him the truth, I mean. About the wrong address."

Savage felt the weight of that settle in his chest. He'd called him two days ago and told him the news. It hadn't been an easy conversation. The young man had sat very still for a long time, and then he'd said, very quietly, that he was glad to know. That not knowing would have been worse.

Savage wasn't sure he believed that, but he respected the choice.

"Most of the community's going," Barb went on. "Grace from the book club is organizing the reception at the Methodist hall afterwards. The vets' center is sending a contingent. Commissioner Albright's name has been quietly removed from the program."

"Good," Savage said.

"I'll be there," Sinclair said.

"Me too," Lucas added.

Thorpe nodded without speaking.

"We'll all go," Savage said. "Dress uniform."

Barb gave a small, satisfied nod and went back to her desk.

Sinclair cleared her throat. "While we're all standing around, there's actually one more thing."

She picked up a pile of envelopes off of her desk and began handing them out. By the time she reached Savage, she was holding the last one, and she handed it over with a small, almost embarrassed smile.

"Mason and I set a date," she said. "Spring. The lodge up at Vallecito, before the tourists arrive. We'd like you all to come."

Savage turned the envelope over in his hand. His name was written across the front in neat blue ink.

"About time," Lucas grinned.

"Watch it," Sinclair shot back, but she was smiling too.

Thorpe was already turning his envelope over with the focused interest of a man examining evidence. "Is there a plus-one?"

"Yes, Thorpe. There's a plus-one."

"Good to know."

Savage tucked the save-the-date notification into the inside pocket of his jacket. "Congratulations, Sinclair. Mason's a lucky man."

She turned and smiled at him. "Thanks, boss."

HE LEFT the office a little after eleven.

He'd told Barb he was heading out for the rest of the day, and she hadn't asked where. She'd just nodded and said she'd hold any calls. That was the thing about Barb. She always seemed to know when to ask and when not to.

Outside, the air was sharp and clean, the kind of late autumn morning that promised a hard winter not far behind. The hills above town were bare now, the last of the aspen gold long since stripped away by the wind. The scars from the summer fires were still there along the ridge, but for the first time that he could remember, they didn't feel like the only thing he saw when he looked at them.

He climbed into the Suburban that Barb had requisitioned. It was a newer model than his old one, and it still smelled of plastic and cleaning product. He'd get used to it.

He sat for a moment with his hands on the wheel.

He'd made the decision sometime during the night, lying awake watching the ceiling, going over the last conversation with Becca for the hundredth time. The cold goodbye. The way he'd hung up. *Give Connor my love.* Like he was already on the outside of his own family.

He wasn't going to do that.

He thought about Quentin Wilson, sitting in that motel room, hearing that the parents he'd spent three years angry at had died because of a typo on a GPS. About all those years he couldn't get back. About a letter from an aunt he'd never met that had taken everything he thought he knew and turned it sideways.

He thought about Harrow, sitting with twenty years of guilt because he'd trusted the wrong man and walked into a house that wasn't empty.

He thought about Frank and Sarah Wilson, who hadn't even been the target.

Life was too damn short to let the people you loved drift away just because you were too proud to fight for them.

He'd drive up to Pagosa Springs. Tonight, if he could. Tomorrow at the latest. He would sit down with Becca and tell her what he should have told her on the phone three nights ago. That he didn't accept it. That whoever this person was, he wasn't the father of her son, and he wasn't the man who knew her real name and he wasn't going to lose her without a fight. Savage was prepared to do whatever it took. Move. Resign, if she asked him to. Find a way back, however long it took.

He'd rehearsed none of it. He didn't need to. The words would come or they wouldn't.

But first, there was somewhere he needed to be.

He started the engine, pulled out of the lot, and turned west onto the road that led out of town toward the foothills. Past the hardware store, past the elementary school, past the turnoff for Maple Ridge Lane. The traffic was light. The sky was wide and pale and clear.

Twenty minutes later, he turned onto the long gravel drive that led up to Jasmine Hatch's farm. Smoke rose from the chimney, soft and grey against the morning. The porch light was off. The kitchen window glowed a warm yellow.

He killed the engine and sat for a moment, listening to the tick of it cooling.

Then he climbed out, settled his hat on his head, and walked up to the door.

The story continues in Snow Burn. Grab your copy today!
https://a.co/d/0glaNCIY

Join the L.T. Ryan reader family & receive a free copy of the Rachel Hatch story, *Fractured*. Click the link below to get started: https://ltryan.com/rachel-hatch-newsletter-signup-1

Join the L.T. Ryan private reader's group on Facebook here: https://www.facebook.com/groups/1727449564174357

ALSO BY L.T. RYAN

Find All of L.T. Ryan's Books on Amazon Today!

<u>The Jack Noble Series</u>

The Recruit (free)

The First Deception (Prequel 1)

Noble Beginnings

A Deadly Distance

Ripple Effect (Bear Logan)

Thin Line

Noble Intentions

When Dead in Greece

Noble Retribution

Noble Betrayal

Never Go Home

Beyond Betrayal (Clarissa Abbot)

Noble Judgment

Never Cry Mercy

Deadline

End Game

Noble Ultimatum

Noble Legend

Noble Revenge

Never Look Back

The Devil's Bargain

Noble Reckoning

Bear Logan Series

Ripple Effect

Blowback

Take Down

Deep State

Bear & Mandy Logan Series

Close to Home

Under the Surface

The Last Stop

Over the Edge

Between the Lies

Caught in the Web

The Marked Daughter

Beneath the Frozen Sky

What the Fog Hides

Rachel Hatch Series

Drift

Downburst

Fever Burn

Smoke Signal

Firewalk

Whitewater

Aftershock

Whirlwind

Tsunami

Fastrope

Sidewinder

Redaction

Mirage

Faultline

Switchback

Mitch Tanner Series

The Depth of Darkness

Into The Darkness

Deliver Us From Darkness

Cassie Quinn Series

Path of Bones

Whisper of Bones

Symphony of Bones

Etched in Shadow

Concealed in Shadow

Betrayed in Shadow

Born from Ashes

Return to Ashes

Risen from Ashes

Into the Light

Blake Brier Series

Unmasked

Unleashed

Uncharted

Drawpoint

Contrail

Detachment

Clear

Quarry

Dalton Savage Series

Savage Grounds

Scorched Earth

Cold Sky

The Frost Killer

Crimson Moon

Dust Devil

Savage Season

Snow Burn

Maddie Castle Series

The Handler

Tracking Justice

Hunting Grounds

Vanished Trails

Smoldering Lies

Field of Bones

Beneath the Grove

Disappearing Act

Silent Witness

Affliction Z Series

Affliction Z: Patient Zero

Affliction Z: Abandoned Hope

Affliction Z: Descended in Blood

Affliction Z : Fractured Part 1

Affliction Z: Severed

Affliction Z: Dead Reckoning

Alex Hayes Series

Trial By Fire (Prequel)

Fractured Verdict

11th Hour Witness

Buried Testimony

The Bishop's Recusal

The Silent Gavel

Improper Influence

Stella LaRosa Series

Black Rose

Red Ink

Black Gold

White Lies

Silver Bullet

Avril Dahl Series

Cold Reckoning

Cold Legacy

Cold Mercy

Savannah Shadows Series

Echoes of Guilt

The Silence Before

Dead Air

Danny Cortez Series

Dead Man's List

Shadow Directive

Widow Protocol

Jane Cannon Series

Blind Trust

Collateral

Gwen Kane Series

Victim or Villain

Hunted or Hunter

Receive a free copy of The Recruit. Visit:

https://ltryan.com/jack-noble-newsletter-signup-1

THE DALTON SAVAGE SERIES

Savage Grounds

Scorched Earth

Cold Sky

The Frost Killer

Crimson Moon

Dust Devil

Savage Season

Snow Burn

Join the L.T. Ryan reader family & receive a free copy of the Rachel Hatch story, *Fractured*. Click the link below to get started:

https://ltryan.com/rachel-hatch-newsletter-signup-1

ABOUT THE AUTHOR

L.T. RYAN is a *Wall Street Journal*, *USA Today*, and Amazon bestselling author of several mysteries and thrillers, including the *Wall Street Journal* bestselling Jack Noble and Rachel Hatch series. With over eight million books sold, when he's not penning his next adventure, L.T. enjoys traveling, hiking, riding his Peloton,, and spending time with his wife, daughter and four dogs at their home in central Virginia.

* Sign up for his newsletter to hear the latest goings on and receive some free content → https://ltryan.com/jack-noble-newsletter-signup-1
* Join LT's private readers' group → https://www.facebook.com/groups/1727449564174357
* Follow on Instagram → @ltryanauthor
* Visit the website → https://ltryan.com
* Send an email → contact@ltryan.com
* Find on Goodreads → http://www.goodreads.com/author/show/6151659.L_T_Ryan

---

BIBA PEARCE is a British crime writer and author of the Kenzie Gilmore, Dalton Savage and DCI Rob Miller series.

Biba grew up in post-apartheid Southern Africa. As a child, she lived on the wild eastern coast and explored the sub-tropical forests and surfed in shark-infested waters.

Now a full-time writer, Biba lives in leafy Surrey and when she isn't writing, can be found walking through the countryside or kayaking on the river Thames.

Visit her at bibapearce.com and join her mailing list to be notified about new releases, updates and special subscriber-only deals.

www.ingramcontent.com/pod-product-compliance
Lightning Source LLC
LaVergne TN
LVHW010609100826
845148LV00014B/2901

* 9 7 8 1 6 8 5 3 3 5 1 5 1 *